Evil At

SHORE HAVEN

Also by Alice Zogg

Stand-Alone Mystery
A Bet Turned Deadly

R. A. Huber Mysteries

Guilty or Not
Murder at the Cubbyhole
Revamp Camp
Final Stop Albuquerque
The Fall of Optimum House
The Lonesome Autocrat
Tracking Backward
Turn the Joker Around
Reaching Checkmate

Evil At
SHORE HAVEN

Alice Zogg

Published by Aventine Press
55 East Emerson St.
Chula Vista CA 91911
www.aventinepress.com

ISBN: 978-1-59330-911-4

Library of Congress Control Number: 2016913554
Library of Congress Cataloging-in-Publication Data
EVIL AT SHORE HAVEN/Alice Zogg
Printed in the United States of America

In memory of Eunice, my friend of five decades

CREDITS

Credit is due to Karen Carter, who parted with valued information about retirement communities. Thank you, Karen, for taking the time and effort to educate me on the complex subject of retirement living. Stan Carter gave tips on a mixed-doubles tennis match. I appreciate your expertise, Stan. As with every book, I relied on my daughter Franziska's proofreading skills. How wonderful to have such a gem in the family! Again, Valoise Douglas applied herself to a superb editing job. Last, but not least, I thank my husband, Wilfried, for his readiness to explore locations with me. For researching this book, he accompanied me on a trip to Utah and helped scout out a Ventura beach for the setting of my fictional retirement community.

CAST OF CHARACTERS

R. A. Huber Ex-private investigator; acting as consultant

Peter Huber R. A. Huber's husband; a writer

Antoinette LeJeune (Andi) Huber's former assistant; now running the show

Carla & Kirk Ralph A couple; they hire Andi to investigate Shore Haven

Kitty Ralph Kirk's mother; drowned in the ocean

Dave Beaulieu Executive director of Shore Haven; efficient

Bea Guinto In house LVN nurse; a no-nonsense woman

Caitlyn Novark Front desk receptionist; young, pleasant, and cute

Dr. Wang Physician available to residents; comes once a week

Emilia Munoz Maintenance director; rules over her domestic staff with an iron fist

Hailey Sparks Activity coordinator; always chipper

Minerva Moore One of the caregivers; has a knack with handling old folks

Jim and Jane	Residents; married for over four decades but keep their romance going
Tom	Resident; has caught the attention of the ladies
Bill	Resident; a great athlete
Rose	Resident: a mute who keeps her eyes wide open
Cheryl	Resident; not above a bit of gossip
Elaine	Resident; loves to sing, although not always on key
Todd	Elaine's nephew; known among residents as "the nice young man"
Betty	Resident; the oldest boarder, yet sharper than most
Claudia	Resident; keeps her celebrity status under wraps
Charley	Assisted resident; can be difficult if provoked

PROLOGUE

Two figures trekked through the sand toward the water.

"Ready for your first swimming lesson?" the taller one asked.

"I am," old Kitty Ralph replied. And with a sudden sparkle in her eyes she added, "My bathing suit sure is pretty!"

"I'm glad you like it. You're keeping this our little secret, right?"

She nodded and said, "Everyone will be surprised that I can swim!"

"Let's hurry up, then, before it gets too dark to see the waves coming. I promise, we won't go in farther than where you can comfortably stand."

At sunset, there was no one else near the ocean by Shore Haven's stretch of beach on this mild, early March evening. They left their towels and flip flops on the sand, carefully watched their steps when treading over the rocks, and then waded in the shallow water, holding hands. Kitty shivered when the frigid Pacific reached her thighs.

"Just a few steps farther and the instructions can begin," the other person coaxed.

When the first breaker reached them, Kitty felt a push. She screamed and swallowed some water. She was still coughing when the second wave rolled along, and it was easy to hold her under and keep her there; she barely weighed 105 pounds. The old woman scarcely put up a struggle, and it was over with in no time.

As the last glimmers of the vanishing sun against the horizon reflected on the surface of the ocean, a lone figure scrambled out of the water and over the strip of rocks, tossed Kitty's flip flops and towel into the nearest trash bin, and then walked casually away along the sandy shore.

CHAPTER 1

Andi parked her Harley-Davidson in the lot and then took the few yards with long, cowboy-booted strides to the two-story building on North Lake Avenue in Pasadena. Her office was at ground level. *Her* office! she mused. Two years into the venture, the young woman was still amazed by the fact. The sign "R. A. Huber, Private Detective" had long been replaced by another that read "Antoinette LeJeune & R. A. Huber, Private Investigators." Andi stood looking at the shingle for a second and thought, Holy Krewe, that's me! Then she quickly turned the key in the lock and let herself in.

She took off her helmet, shook the wavy, auburn hair loose, and hung her black leather jacket on the office chair's backrest. She then settled at the desk for some secretarial chores, mainly typing up a bill for a recently solved case. The task would have to wait. She had scarcely entered her password into the desktop computer when new clients, a husband and wife, appeared at her door.

The man took one look at Andi and said, "We need to deal with the older lady. Is she in?"

"R. A. Huber?"

"Yes, her."

"Mrs. Huber is retired and only occasionally acts as my consultant. I'm Antoinette LeJeune, qualifyin' with a private investigator license; gun permit and all. How may I help you folks?"

They gave the young woman with the Southern drawl a skeptical look, and the man said, "I doubt that you can."

There was a long pause and then he said, "My name is Kirk Ralph, and this is my wife, Carla. The Huber lady came highly recommended, but since she is not available, we might as well tell you our plight. My mother was a resident at Shore Haven and drowned in the ocean. The authorities concluded that it was an accidental drowning, but we think that she was murdered."

"Where and what is Shore Haven?" Andi asked.

"It's a retirement community about a mile north of the Ventura pier. The place is located right by the ocean."

"Go on."

Kirk continued, "The idea is that Mom did not remember that she couldn't swim, took a dip in the ocean one evening last month, and drowned."

"That's absurd," Andi said. "How could she forget such a thing? Oh, I get it. Was she mentally disabled?"

"She had been recently diagnosed with Alzheimer's, but the illness was in its early stage. There is no way on earth that she thought she could swim. Mom was afraid of water and never went near the pool, let alone put as much as her little toe into the ocean. She didn't even own a bathing suit; someone must have given her the one she was wearing when they found her."

"Hold on," Andi interjected. "Tell me everything you know about the drowning in chronological order, please."

"There isn't much to tell. Mom was missed at dinner and when she was nowhere to be found on the premises, Mr. Beaulieu - - that's the man who runs Shore Haven - - organized a search party around the neighborhood and along the beach. Mom did not sign herself out at the front desk, and her car was still parked in the parking structure. The idea was that she wandered off on foot. We were not there but learned about it after the fact. Anyway, the search was useless and the authorities got involved, treating it as a missing person case. Three days later, someone found her washed up near the pier."

Carla shuddered and said, "It was horrible. We had to identify her body at the morgue. She was grotesque, all bloated."

Her husband patted her shoulder and said, "Try not to dwell on that." And turning back to Andi, he stated, "I want justice for Mom, but we can't go to the police since we have no evidence of foul play."

"Who do you think murdered her?"

"We have no idea."

"Did your mama make enemies?"

"Certainly not!" he shot back. "She was a gentle soul; everyone liked her."

Andi scratched her head and said, "You can't have it both ways, sir. Either someone had a reason to kill your mama, or else she drowned by accident."

"Maybe she found out what's going on at Shore Haven and needed to be silenced," Carla suggested.

Andi's radar was on alert now and she prompted, "Say what?"

"About two weeks before she passed, Mom told us that residents were dying at a rapid rate. In her own words, 'People are dropping dead right and left around here.'"

"Isn't that normal at an old folks home?"

"That's what we thought at the time she made the comment. Now we feel differently."

"Y'all think there's a mercy killer on the loose?"

"Not really. Some of these people were not all that old and in relatively good health."

"If you worried about her safety, how come you didn't take her out of there?" Andi wanted to know.

Kirk replied, "First off, I'd like to point out that Shore Haven is a top notch facility and Mom was happy there. Until her drowning, we didn't put much importance to her remark. To be fair, she did tend to get things mixed up. After she passed, we talked to a resident she had befriended and learned of the recent deaths at the facility. Granted, some of these people most likely died from natural causes, but others did not, in our opinion. The fatalities seem natural or accidental at first glance, but something fishy is going on below the surface."

Andi grabbed her notepad and pen, inquiring "What is the friend's name?"

"We only know her first name, Cheryl."

"Do you suspect that management or staff members are involved in any wrong doing, or is it other old folks you're concerned about?"

"We haven't got a clue."

Whenever Andi got excited, frustrated, angry, or didn't know what to say, her southern drawl became acute. She was clearly at a loss for words when she probed, "What'd y'all have me doin'?"

"Investigate the place, of course," Kirk said.

Andi mulled things over. She was by no means convinced that there *was* something to investigate. After all, the old woman was going off her rocker and most likely had forgotten that she could not swim and ambled into the ocean of her own free will.

She finally said, "If I show up at the community's doorstep asking questions, I'll be thrown out like a common beggar, for sure. You reckon I apply for a job at the place? I doubt that I'd come up with proper qualifications."

"That is exactly why we wanted to hire the older lady. She could check in as a resident."

Andi raised an eyebrow and asked, "You would pay for her stay?"

"Naturally."

Andi looked him straight in the eye and said, "You're sure your mama's drowning was not an accident?"

"Positive."

His wife remarked, "Who in their right mind would even want to venture into the freezing ocean at the beginning of March?"

Andi thought, that's just it, the woman was not in her right mind. And as far as venturing into the ocean in March, surfers, divers, and gung-ho swimmers did it all the time, even in the midst of winter. She kept those thoughts to herself, however.

"I'll see what I can do," she said and took down data, such as their phone number, address, and other personal information.

"And now," she stated, "I need to know lots more about Shore Haven before we can go on."

CHAPTER 2

Peter Huber shut his laptop with a bang and cried out, "It's no use. I give up!"

R. A. Huber looked up from the Far East travel brochure she had been studying and said, "What's eating you?"

"I've revised this damned paragraph for the hundredth time and it still doesn't read right. That's what."

"Maybe if I had a look at the entire chapter, I could help."

His good humor restored, he laughed and said, "Regula, I can't believe that you're still determined to get a peek at my manuscripts after all these years of my writing career."

"You can't blame a gal for trying."

They were seated on the living room recliners at their home in the town of Merida, located in the San Fernando Valley at the foot of the Angeles National Forest Mountains. The pair carried their age well. New silver strands showed on the woman's salt-and-pepper hair, pulled away from her brow in a becoming style, and a few more laugh lines adorned her face. These signs were evidence of a life lived to the fullest. She was still trim and the athletic spring to her gait had not diminished. Her husband's hair had long turned snow white, and even the prominent eyebrows and mustache seemed to lighten with each new day, but his hazel eyes were forever steady and held strength of character.

Peter looked at his spouse of many decades and remarked, "Did I ever tell you that I'm relieved you quit the investigating business?"

"A few times!"

"I can't help it. After one of your murderers tried to silence you and I watched for days as you lay in the hospital unconscious, not knowing if you'd ever come out of the coma, you can't blame me for being thrilled that you gave it up."

"Yeah, I guess it was time. I do miss the action, though. Andi is holding her own, which I knew she would." With a sigh, she added, "She consults me less and less; good for her yet bittersweet for me."

They kept silent, each lost in their own musings. The lady thought back to that first day Andi had blown into her office like a whirlwind. The 18-year-old's mischievous green eyes had peered at her, asking "Can y'all use any help 'round here?" When bidden to share a bit of her background, Huber learned that the young woman's mother had died while giving birth to her and that she had been brought up by her daddy in New Orleans, where he owned a bar in the French Quarter. He had taught her how to play the fiddle, dance the Cajun Waltz, fish, ride the Harley, load - shoot - and take care of a gun, as well as cook gumbo and jambalaya. Prior to showing up at Huber's private investigating business, Andi's daddy had passed away, and she had ridden to California on her Harley-Davidson. In addition to the motorcycle, Daddy had also left her three pieces; a hunting rifle, which she had sold to a pawn shop, a Derringer and a Stinger pen pistol, which were still in her possession.

A few months later, she had sent the spunky young woman from New Orleans undercover to Optimum House, where she had proved herself worthy to become Huber's assistant. That was nearly eight years ago. Meanwhile, Andi had earned her bachelor degree at UCLA and was running the investigating business now.

Peter's thoughts had reverted back to his current manuscript and he almost jumped when the phone rang on the end table next to him. He glanced at it and, as he checked caller-ID, announced, "Speak of the devil," handing the phone over to his spouse.

"How're y'all doin', Mrs. Huber?"

"Hello Andi! What's up?"

"Do you have time to talk?"

"All the time in the world; I'm retired!"

"Well, boss - -"

"I'm no longer your boss!"

"I keep forgettin'. Anyhow, are you up to tackle some active detecting? I'd like to send you on an undercover job."

Huber snickered and said, "Sounds like our roles are truly reversed now, but go ahead and clue me in."

So Andi related what she had learned from the Ralph couple that morning, ending with, "I know that we don't have much to go on, but I'd like to give it a try. I asked them who inherits old Mrs. Ralph's money. They were offended by the question but answered it. There are some minor legacies, but the bulk of her fortune goes to them." And she added, "I got the feelin' that the pair is not starving as is. He's a CEO in a major electronics company, and she's a professor, lecturing at USC."

"Looks like you asked all the right questions. I taught you well. Did you believe their claim that some of the old folks had been killed rather than died naturally?"

"There is no doubt in their minds, but I don't know what to believe. The authorities seemed satisfied that the residents died of illness or old age when signing the death certificates. There was one accident, besides Kitty Ralph's drowning. The couple didn't know any details, but apparently one old lady fell down a flight of stairs and died of her injuries. I reckon you'll get at the truth if you agree to the assignment."

"Are you trying to butter me up?"

"Yes, ma'am."

"And you said the Ralphs will pick up the tab if I check myself in as a boarder?"

"Yes, ma'am, but I believe the term is 'resident.'"

"This retirement community is in Ventura, you said?"

"That's right. By the beach, about a mile north of the pier."

R. A. Huber thought aloud, "Only a little more than an hour's drive from my house." And she asked, "The place is posh?"

"You bet! Privately owned, and I believe a corporation. Has its own tennis court, beach access, and indoor swimming pool. It obviously houses seniors who can afford luxury in their golden years."

"Peter isn't going to be happy if I accept the job."

"Tell Mr. Huber that I'll check with you daily, and if there's any trouble, I'll show up with my Derringer in a flash."

Her ex-boss laughed and said, "That would make him worry even more!"

After some consideration she announced, "Okay, I'll do it, under the condition that I will not accept payment for the job."

Andi protested, "I can't let you work for free."

"I won't be hurting. You, on the other hand, have to make a living from the investigating business. So do we have an agreement?"

"Yes, ma'am. And thank you kindly."

"If it turns out to be nothing but a wild goose chase, at least I'll have a pleasant retirement experience near the ocean."

"Thank you again for accepting the job. Come by the office tomorrow morning and we'll figure out the details."

As predicted, Peter was irritated when he learned of his wife's decision.

"Dammit Regula!" he shouted, "Isn't it a fact that you gave up active duty for good? Why expose yourself to danger again?"

"Give me some credit. I ought to be capable of handling an old folks place without much damage to myself," she replied with a chuckle.

He shot her an angry look and stated, "It's not funny. I hate the idea!"

CHAPTER 3

Who would have thought that checking into a retirement community would involve so much red tape and hassle? R. A. Huber soon became familiar with the scrutiny involved. The process of applying for residency at Shore Haven took over two weeks, starting with her filling out an Application for Residency form, then signing a 40-page long contract, and many State forms. She also needed to have a seven-page State Physicians Report completed, which included a TB test. She was lucky to have had a complete physical at the beginning of the year, so that her own doctor took care of that requirement and filled out the report.

Huber tried to stick to the truth as much as possible when putting down information on the application forms, giving her own name and address, birthdate, et cetera, but some omissions and deviations from the truth could not be avoided. For instance, in the field, "previous occupation" she put "secretary." It was correct that when starting her private investigating business a dozen years ago, she had been a retired secretary. The one outright lie she was guilty of had to do with her status. She wrote down that she was recently widowed and scared to live in her house alone. Peter would never forgive her for this shameful fib, but how else was she going to state a plausible reason for applying to the retirement facility? For "emergency contact #1" she named Andi, listing her as distant relative. As to "emergency contact #2", good old friend Peggy had the honors. She left emergency contacts #3 and #4 blank. The last two pages of the application asked for financial information. Huber inflated her assets to numbers that would justify her stay at the upscale retirement community, hoping that nobody would bother checking the details.

She paid the required non-refundable deposit, covered by funds Kirk Ralph had deposited into her checking account. Bea Guinto, the nurse, grilled Huber on some memory questions to determine her mental capacity, which helped the executive director, Dave Beaulieu, establish what level of residency she was to be assigned to.

At the beginning of the mental testing, Ms. Guinto asked Huber to memorize three unrelated words - - i.e., peach, ball, and book - - and recall them 15 minutes later at the end of the session. The time in between was reserved for questions like, "What town are we in?" "In what state is that?" "What is today's date?" and so forth. Then followed some math: "Please subtract from 100 backward in segments of 7." The nurse stopped Huber when she got to 65. There was also a visual test where she was shown a sketch of a simple geometric design of a few lines. She then was given paper and pen and asked to copy the easy drawing. It was clear that the dark-haired woman from the Philippines had no time or patience for nonsense. She was not amused when Huber joked, "For how much will you sell my artwork?"

Shore Haven offered two resident categories, the independent and the assisted living. Each group was housed in separate wings of the facility and had their own dining room. In order to qualify as an independent

resident, one had to be able to take care of oneself. The fire
and state laws dictated that a person must be able to get
out of the building in an emergency without help. And, of
course, you had to be mentally fit. Assisted living residents
may need medication management, help with bathing or
dressing, may forget to come to meals, have problems of
incontinence, a large amount of memory loss, or all of the
above.

As expected, Huber was to reside with the independents.
She was given the choice of a two-bedroom, one-bedroom,
or studio with kitchenette apartment, each coming with
its own price tag. Mr. Beaulieu mentioned the existence
of a couple of three-bedroom suites on the topmost floor,
but that both were being occupied at the moment. She
opted for the studio, not taking needless advantage of the
Ralphs' generosity.

As for rent, there were two options. The first was the so-
called buy-in, with a six-figure initial down payment, where
the monthly rent was reduced to 30%, and a guarantee of
care if the person's money ran out. The alternative was
a month-to-month set rent, which increased yearly, and
there was no care guarantee. With both options, a non-
refundable opening fee was mandatory. Logically, Huber
chose the month-to-month deal.

"You can choose a meal plan," said Mr. Beaulieu, "full
three meals a day or two meals or one meal, or even no
meals at all. The rent is based on how many meals you
wish to eat at Shore Haven. We provide restaurant-style
dining, and our meals are nutritious and tasty."

Huber pondered this for a second, then decided to
go full speed ahead. Sharing meals together was a great
opportunity to get into residents' heads. She said, "Sign
me up for all meals."

"Good choice, Regula!" And he added, "I hope you
don't mind our first name policy. At Shore Haven, we

don't bother with residents' last names. It's a lot easier on everybody."

Cringing at his pronunciation, Huber replied, "My first name is a mouthful for most Americans."

"What does your middle initial stand for?"

"Agatha, which I personally dislike. How about just calling me R. A.?"

"That works," and he scribbled, "Wants to be called R. A." on one of the forms.

Getting back to the former subject, he continued, "On the days you are away for meals, you must call the front desk or kitchen to cancel. You can add guests at mealtimes whenever you like but need to sign them in at the front desk and specify, 'Add to bill or pay cash.'"

She inquired, "Do you offer furnished apartments?"

Mr. Beaulieu replied, "Not officially. Most residents like to bring their own furniture. But we can throw something together, if you like."

"I'm not ready to sell my house yet and don't want to move my things out in case I decide to go back, if I'm not happy here."

He smiled at her and said, "I understand. We keep a storage room full of former residents' furniture. Come, I'll show you." And as they both got up, he added, "I was planning to give you a tour of our community anyway."

Her tour guide was in his forties, clean-shaven, with short, straight brown hair in a neat cut. He wore a suit and tie and polished dress shoes. R. A. did not detect a single stray stubble at the back of his neck as she followed him out of his office. The man seemed to live and breathe efficiency.

Pointing right and left, he stated, "These are the staff offices and you've already met Caitlyn Novark, one of our receptionists at the front desk. She directs residents to the proper staff person with their problems and requests. The front desk is the hub of our community. State laws require residents to sign themselves and possible guests in and out as they come and go."

R. A. nodded.

"I assume you parked in the underground garage, so you already know that residents and visitors alike need to record their license plate numbers at the front desk?"

She nodded again.

As they stepped past Ms. Novark's domain, R. A. noticed an elderly couple with golf gear signing themselves out at her desk. She heard the cute young receptionist say to them, "Don't kill all the birdies!"

They bypassed the loading dock, and as Mr. Beaulieu opened the door to the storage room, he said, "You don't have to decide now, but pick whatever furniture you wish and then let one of our maintenance people know and they'll move the items to your studio. The only thing we don't have available is beds. You'll need to bring your own, as there is a law that does not allow used beds."

They walked on and stopped at the lounge, which was a large room decked out with couches, chairs, game card tables, and a long desk with several desktop computers next to one wall. Against another stood shelf cases housing board games like chess, checkers, backgammon, and monopoly, as well as dominos, pick-up-sticks, playing cards and some hi-tech toys. There was a woman hovering over a desktop PC. Huber was unsure if she was doing research on the internet or playing a computer game. A couple of other residents were watching the news on a big screen T.V.

Her guide said, "Our lounge is where all residents mingle and socialize or just relax. This is where our activity coordinator, Hailey Sparks, organizes entertainment, such as BINGO, concerts, and talent shows. There isn't much going on in here at this time of the day, but before and after dinner the lounge gets jumping." And he added, "If you have any special expertise or talent, talk to Ms. Sparks. She's always looking for new forms of entertainment."

Next door was the library, and adjacent to that, an elegant little room serving as café and tea room, named Tiki Bar. The Polynesian décor with its bamboo plants, indoor fountain, and murals of palm trees, sandy beaches, and hula girls gave the place a romantic touch. There were several old folks sipping their mid-morning tea or coffee. Some looked up and smiled, while others did not seem to notice the Executive Director with the new resident.

An open passage from the Tiki Bar led to the play room, which had game tables, like ping pong and foosball, but without a doubt, the main attraction was a standard-size pool table. R. A. was impressed.

Mr. Beaulieu gave her a quick peek into the chapel, which stood as a separate small structure between the independent residential and the assisted living buildings. The modest house of worship was flanked by rows of fragrant white gardenia shrubs. About 20 yards behind the chapel was the fenced-in tennis court and next to it the indoor swimming pool. After passing the chapel once more, they walked straight to the large building that housed the independent residents.

Before they entered it, he pointed across a covered connecting passageway and said, "That leads to the assisted living wing, which you most likely will not get to experience. They have their separate dining room."

As he guided her through the ground floor of the independents building - - showing her the laundry room, a spa and hair salon, a gym with workout equipment, and the pleasant-looking dining room - - Huber felt confident that she would enjoy her stay.

"And now," he said, "let me show you the studio we have available for you."

On the elevator ride up to the fourth floor, he informed her that there were five stories, housing up to 50 independent residents, whereas the building across the walkway had only two floors with 20 assisted living folks. He added, "Naturally, residents confined to a wheelchair or the ones needing multiple assistance reside on the ground floor. We have a staff of compassionate caregivers in the assisted living wing. Should you at some time in the future need special care, we'll make sure that the transition and relocation to those living quarters will be made easy and smooth for you."

Huber's soon-to-be studio was a corner room with a view of the beach. The kitchenette appeared to be miniscule, but then she only planned to brew coffee or tea in it. She surveyed the empty space and tried to visualize a few pieces of furniture she had spotted in the storeroom as a possible fit. A glance into the bathroom met with her approval. Tub, sink, and toilet all looked squeaky clean. Then she went out onto the balcony and looked down to the ocean. She saw a yacht gliding over the calm sea in the distance. On shore, she observed a jogger parallel to the water's edge and a couple of figures ambling slowly along the walkway between her building and the stretch of sand leading to the ocean. She thought of poor Mrs. Ralph and almost jumped, when the man standing behind her said, "The beach is our most sought-after asset!"

Later, as R. A. drove out of the facility's underground garage, she thought, *I'm in, and so far, no one has singled me out as an imposter.*

At the same time Dave Beaulieu sat in his office and rehashed the orientation meeting he had just completed. The woman had been straightforward enough, yet, there was something about her that suggested a red flag. He couldn't put his finger on it, though, and decided he was probably mistaken.

CHAPTER 4

Peter was still mad at his spouse and wanted nothing to do with her move. She purchased a cheap twin bed plus bedding, having it delivered, and Andi helped her with the rest of the move, mainly a few suitcases filled with things that would keep her going for about a month. She could have easily handled the luggage on her own but asked Andi along for comfort and company. It also seemed a good idea to familiarize the young woman with the territory, since she was the head investigator.

Besides the bed, Huber's studio apartment now was furnished with a nightstand, a mirror-dresser, an Ottoman chair plus end table, and a 24" TV. Nothing matched, but the items were functional. There was a built-in wall safe, and after reading the instructions, she programed it with a new six-digit code. She then took her .25 pistol out of her purse and placed it into the safe.

Andi had followed her former boss to Ventura in the Harley-Davidson, and after settling into her apartment at Shore Haven, Huber took her on a tour of the grounds.

Before they headed out the studio door, she warned, "Don't call me Mrs. Huber while on this assignment. I've listed you as a distant relative."

"I'll call you Auntie. Okay?"

"Perfect!"

Andi was captivated with the tennis court, the indoor swimming pool, and the spacious lounge, but what really blew her away was the playroom.

She exclaimed, "Holy Krewe! I'd be tickled pink if I were you, Auntie."

The two men shooting pool halted their game and the blue-eyed one said, "The name's Tom, and my buddy is Bill." And addressing Huber he continued, "With whom do we have the pleasure?"

"I'm R. A., and Andi helped me move here."

"Welcome!" Then he took in Andi's unruly auburn hair, long legs clad in skinny jeans, leather jacket and cowboy boots. He beamed at her, saying, "We don't see enough young things around here. You, my dear, are a real treat for sore eyes."

"Thank you, sir!"

"Is that a motorcycle helmet hanging from your bag?"

"Yes, sir. I ride a Harley."

"I'm impressed. And you're a Southern Belle to boot! Tell me, what 'holy' something did you refer to when you first came in?"

"Oh that!" Embarrassed, she explained, "Sometimes I can't help myself when I get excited. A Krewe is an organization that parades at Mardi Gras."

Bill, who was bald and had an athlete's body, did not say a word, but impatiently chalked his cue stick, antsy to get back to the game.

Huber apologized, "We didn't mean to intrude. Good shooting to you both," and she eased Andi out of the playroom.

Minutes later, they were strolling on the pathway along the senior community's buildings to their right, and the beach on the left. They observed several people, presumably residents, promenading themselves or sitting on the property's beachfront benches on that fine afternoon in April. The ocean scene was peaceful and tranquil. They soon engaged in shoptalk, taking advantage of their outdoor privacy.

Andi said, "Everything we've seen and heard so far is sweet and proper, and the place seems a haven, justifying its name."

"I agree," said Huber. "It will take time to dig underneath the surface. And if the digging gets me nowhere, you can assure the Ralphs that we tried. I'll interview everyone concerned, without them realizing that they're being interviewed."

"You're good at that! At my end, I'll do a background check on each person, soon as you give me their names."

"For starters, I can give you the names of the executive director, the in-house LVN nurse, and the front desk receptionist. Getting last names of residents might be a problem. The head honcho informed me the other day that they only go by their first names."

Andi, full of confidence, stated, "You'll think of somethin', no doubt." Then she said, "Best call or text me when you have info, not the other way around. I don't want to interrupt talks you may have with suspects."

"Strictly speaking, they're not suspects yet. We don't know whether any crimes have been committed."

"Yes, ma'am."

They had walked about half a mile and decided to turn around and head back to Shore Haven.

When they got to an unoccupied bench Andi said, "Let's sit and enjoy the ocean view." And pulling an iPad out of her touring bag, she suggested, "How about giving me those names now?"

Huber obliged with the names Dave Beaulieu, Bea Guinto, and Caitlyn Novark, spelling them out letter by letter.

Then she said, "If you want to stay for dinner, I'll sign you in as guest."

"Thank you kindly, but I'd best be headin' home. Oh, I almost forgot" - - she rummaged in her bag and dug out three bright-red skeins of yarn and a pair of knitting needles. "This should keep you busy camouflaging your purpose in this place." she said.

Huber stared at the offering, then burst out laughing.

Before they parted Andi grinned and said, "I'll leave you with the same advice you gave me when sending me off on undercover jobs: *Live the role!*"

CHAPTER 5

R. A. Huber moved in on a Tuesday. Bright and early on Wednesday morning, as she was about ready to head down to the dining room for breakfast, there was a knock at her door. She opened it and faced a young-looking Asian man who was actually 41 years old.

He pushed his glasses farther up his nose and said, "R. A.?"

"Yes. And you are?"

"Dr. Wang. May I come in?"

"Sure," she said, letting him pass by her and closing the door behind him.

Since there was only one chair in her studio, and sitting on her bed seemed awkward, they both remained standing.

"I'm a physician with a medical practice in Ventura. I have committed to taking care of patients at Shore Haven. Every Wednesday morning, I come here to check on my patients." He did his thing with the glasses again and continued, "My visit with you today is because you're a new resident, and as such, I want to make you aware that I can be your doctor, if you wish."

"Thank you, Doctor," she replied, "but there is no need. I am happy with my own physician who gave me a clean bill of health when I had my yearly physical three months ago."

He seemed embarrassed and said, "I totally understand. I introduce myself to all new residents to let them know that I'm available."

"Thanks again, but no thanks."

"Just checking," he said, making a hasty retreat.

Huber thought; did I intimidate the young doctor?

Dr. Wang was riding the elevator down to the ground floor and thought, why did I let myself get rattled by that R. A. person? She's just an old woman, and I'm an established doctor, for crying out loud! In his mind, he replayed the short conversation they'd had and could not recall anything unusual about it. So why the tense feeling? Forget about her, he told himself, as he exited the elevator and walked over to the assisted residents' building to tend to his patients.

Breakfast was buffet style and R. A. helped herself to bacon, scrambled eggs, a piece of toast, and a cup of coffee. That was more food than she was used to eating in the morning, and she hoped that she would still have an appetite at lunch. She shared the breakfast table with a married couple, Jim and Jane, who immediately introduced themselves and welcomed the newcomer into the community. The woman was a youthful appearing blonde, and he, three years her senior, had dark-brown eyes with pure white hair. They both were fit for their ages.

Jane wanted to know, "What does R. A. stand for?"

"I'd rather not say. I dislike my first and middle names, so initials will have to do as we don't use last names."

Jane, who was fast approaching seventy, giggled like a schoolgirl and said, "With us it's the reverse. We prefer our simple first names since Jim's last name is a tongue twister." She leaned close to Huber and whispered it into her ear. The latter paid keen attention, memorizing every syllable.

Then she said, "I saw you the other day at the front desk with your golf gear. Is there a golf course nearby?"

"Only about 10 miles away. Do you play?"

"Occasionally."

Jim said, "We'll take you along on our next round."

"Thanks, but I'm without my clubs; I haven't moved all my stuff yet."

The conversation continued along those lines. They wanted to know if she played tennis. When she told them she'd replaced tennis with racquetball decades ago and that her tennis game was rusty at best, they maintained that playing mixed-doubles would be less challenging. Jim suggested that she partner up with a resident called Bill.

"I've already briefly met someone named Bill. I wonder whether that's him," R. A. remarked.

Jane said, "If he looked like a jock, it must be 'our' Bill." And she giggled again.

The chat then got to more personal matters, and Huber learned that the pair had been married for over four decades and still kept their romance going strong. When they touched on the subject of her own status, she produced a sad face and shared that she was recently widowed.

For some reason that prompted them to finish their last bites of breakfast in a hurry and as they got up Jim said, "We'll organize a match against you and Bill soon. I promise."

The second they were out of sight, Huber slipped her smartphone out of its pocket and stored the couples' last name in her "Notes" application. That one was easy, she mused. Other names may take a bit more finesse to extract.

Then she went for a quick stop to her room to change into flip-flops before heading to the beach. However, she had another visitor.

The woman at her door introduced herself as Emilia Munoz and said, "I'm the maintenance director. I supervise housekeeping and maintenance staff."

"Pleased to meet you."

Emilia was dressed in a black pantsuit and kept her long hair pulled away from her face in a neat bun. The woman seemed to live and breathe authority.

She stated, "The housekeepers clean your room and bath once a week, and the maintenance people are responsible for repairs, upkeep, and they'll assist you with hanging pictures, carrying large packages to your studio, and so forth."

"I've met a couple of the maintenance employees when I selected furniture from your storage room. They did a great job of moving them for me."

"Good to hear. If you find fault with the way your place is cleaned, or if there is any other problem with housekeeping or maintenance, you go through me."

"Understood."

The maintenance director then asked, "Are you planning to do your own laundry, or shall my staff take care of it?"

"I'll do it myself, using the convenient laundry room on the ground floor."

"What about sheets? We have a linen service for that."

"Thanks, but I'll also wash my own sheets."

"As you wish."

Ms. Munoz left and R. A. thought, I wouldn't want to cross that woman if working under her supervision.

The maintenance director decided to take the stairs down to the next floor rather than riding the elevator. She liked to make unannounced spot-checks on her domestic staff. At the moment, they were cleaning the third-floor apartments. As she descended the stairs, she pulled a white glove from her pocked, slipped it over her right hand, and then glided it over the stair railing. Inspecting her gloved hand, she thought, just as I expected: a layer of dust. Someone messed up! I'll see to it, she vowed, and hurried down the last few steps before hunting down her culprit on the third floor.

R. A. noticed a surveillance video camera as she passed through the beach access doors. On the previous day, she had been too preoccupied chatting with Andi to pay attention. This time she did not walk along the path, but headed straight to the ocean. Once on the sand, she slipped off her flip-flops, and carried them barefoot down to the water's edge. She spotted a few surfers farther south, but except for an occasional seagull flying overhead, there was not a soul to be seen at the stretch of beach immediately parallel to Shore Haven. She rolled up her jeans and carefully walked on the strip of rocks between sand and water, and then waded in the shallow ocean. The water felt ice cold. She immediately thought of Mrs. Ralph and that the Pacific had certainly not been any warmer at the beginning of March. Shaking her head, she walked back toward the community grounds.

She sat down on an empty bench and gave her assignment some serious thought. The best way to start her investigation was with old Mrs. Ralph. She mulled over the profile Andi had given her of the lady: age 74, widowed, former columnist of a local paper, in good physical health, recently diagnosed with Alzheimer's. Her late husband was president of a major bank. Kirk is her only child.

About the drowning, she deduced the following: It stood to reason that Mrs. Ralph left the premises of the community alone. Otherwise, the security camera would have caught another person in her company. If she was killed, the murderer was either not a resident or staff member of Shore Haven, or if so, met her at the beach. Her dead body was discovered a few days later, clad in a bathing suit. She must have planned to either lay out on the beach or bathe in the ocean. Both prospects would have made her adventure pretty chilly at the beginning of March. According to her son, the lady did not know how to swim and was afraid of any large body of water, be it a pool, lake, or sea. The theory that she had forgotten that she couldn't swim would have been plausible had Mrs. Ralph suffered from severe dementia, but her son assured Andi that the mental illness was in its early stage.

The whole thing made no sense. Huber sighed and told herself, this is only the first day of my investigation; I'll get at the truth eventually. Then she breathed in the fresh ocean air, listened to the gentle sound of the surf, and enjoyed the idyllic moment.

CHAPTER 6

Lunch on that first day was not productive. Huber found the dining room two-thirds empty. Either she came after the rush, or else most people ate their mid-day meal elsewhere. Whatever the reason, she sat alone at her table. Spending the afternoon in the lounge might have better results, she decided. After all, Mr. Beaulieu had indicated that the lounge was where all the action took place. This was where Andi's idea came into play.

She first went to her room and started her knitting project by casting about 35 stitches onto one of the knitting needles and then created a few rows, to make certain she had not forgotten how. The last time she had knitted was at least 30 years ago when making Peter a sweater. Apparently, the activity was like riding a bike: One never forgot.

In the lounge, she settled into a couch in a strategic position, so that she could watch people coming and going, then knitted away. Amused at Andi's advice to "live the role," she thought, old ladies have come a long way since doing needlework, crocheting, and knitting. By mid-afternoon, the lounge was filling up with folks eager to use the computers, play games, or socialize. A caregiver guided two assisted-living residents - - a man leaning heavily on a walker and a fragile woman on shaky legs - - into the large room, then helped them to chairs at a game table, where she got them started on a game of Dominos.

A woman with short, salt-and-pepper hair and a general air of frailty, walked in, glanced around, and then seated herself on the sofa next to Huber, smiling at her.

"I'm R. A. I moved in yesterday."

The woman smiled again and kept silent, then took a notepad and pen out of her jacket pocket, scribbled on it, and handed it to Huber. It read: "I'm deaf, but can read lips. My name is Rose. Sorry, I could not make out yours."

Huber wrote down, "It's really not a name, just the initials R. A." Then she made sure to face the other and said slowly, "Nice to meet you, Rose," pronouncing every word carefully.

Rose nodded and smiled again, then responded with sign language, which Huber assumed meant "likewise" or something to that effect.

"You'll have to teach me sign language one day when there are less people around."

Rose seemed overjoyed with that prospect and nodded several times. The conversation had run its course and Huber continued knitting, well aware that the other was watching every newcomer to the lounge with interest and appeared to know exactly what went on around her.

Several minutes later, Rose nudged Huber and then showed her the notebook with a new question, "Where are you from?"

"Merida. Located in the San Fernando Valley."

Rose shook her head and wrote, "I mean, originally?"

Huber was flabbergasted! Without hearing, Rose was obviously unable to pick up an accent. She also had no idea about a first or last name. And Huber had been in the US for many decades and had become a citizen ages ago;

therefore, she looked and acted like any given American woman.

She turned to Rose and slowly said, "I was born and raised in Switzerland. How on earth did you suspect that I was not a native of our country?"

"It's the way you knit," she wrote, "it gives away your European origin."

Huber laughed out loud.

There are two styles of knitting - - American versus Continental - - but most people payed no close attention when seeing a person knit. Americans used an arched movement with the hand and fingers, winding the yarn around the needle for each stitch. The Continental, more efficient way to knit was to only use the fingers, keeping both hands straight and winding the yarn around the left index finger in order to get a steady supply of yarn.

The door suddenly flew open and Hailey Sparks made an entrance as if she were on stage. The enthusiastic young woman, clad in a short skirt and knee-high boots, stepped to the center of the room, gazed at the people assembled with fawn eyes, and raised both arms.

"Listen up, everyone! There is still room for tomorrow's excursion to Santa Barbara. So sign up if you haven't already. And tonight is Bingo night, which will be so much fun!"

A couple of people went over to the sign-up roster, but most ignored the cheerful Ms. Sparks, not looking up from whatever they were doing.

She spotted Huber on the couch and made a beeline for her, announcing, "I'm Hailey Sparks, the activity coordinator. You're new, right? What's your name?"

"I go by R. A."

"Just R. A.? Interesting. Well, welcome to Shore Haven, R. A. We provide so many fun activities, you're going to love it here." She gave Huber a sparkling smile, exposing a row of bleached teeth, and added, "If there is anything I can do to make your stay even more enjoyable, be sure to let me know."

With an encompassing wave to everyone in the lounge, the chipper activity coordinator made her exit, saying, "See you all tonight."

R. A. had opted to do straight knitting without any complicated patterns, which enabled her to mostly knit "blind," allowing for observation of her surroundings. Tom entered the lounge, and she was amused to notice that most of the ladies in the room seemed to become alert to the fact. They straightened up, unconsciously arranged a stray strand of hair, tucked at their garments, or freshened up their lipstick.

Tom worked the room and then strutted over to the couch where Rose and R. A. sat. He first leaned over to give Rose a pat on the shoulder and conversed a bit in sign language, then flopped down next to R. A., so that she was seated between them.

He said, "Where is your knockout redhead companion?"

"Andi helped me move yesterday and is long back to her own life."

"Of course. What was I thinking? And you, are you settling in nicely?"

"Just about. There is so much to do here, I won't get bored."

"Judging by the way you've kept your figure, I'd say you'd be interested in the physical activities offered. If you need a guide, I'll show you around," and he winked at her.

Huber didn't care for the man's crude compliment, nor his arrogance, but lived the role and kept the conversation going. She learned that he was a retired architect, had lost his latest wife in a speedboat accident, and joined the retirement community two years ago. He had two sons living out of state, and a daughter who came to visit on rare occasions, without his teenage grandson, who had lost interest in him by about sixth grade. He also shared that he no longer drove but used the Dial-a-Ride service Shore Haven provided to get around.

The man certainly liked to talk and had no problem revealing his life to a stranger. In contrast, R. A. disclosed little of herself. When he asked a direct question about her status, she could not avoid telling him that she was recently widowed. At some point, Rose left them, exchanging some sign language with Tom and ignoring Huber.

CHAPTER 7

Dinner on that Wednesday consisted of vegetable soup, chicken parmesan, green beans, garlic bread, and a choice of cookies, pastry, or fruit from the dessert cart. To R. A.'s pleasant surprise, everything tasted delicious. Management had obviously not held back when hiring the chef. On the previous evening, she had shared a table with Elaine, who had not talked much, using caution by feeling the newcomer out. Elaine, one of the younger residents at 67, was petite, a bit on the chubby side, and in good health. The sole personal thing she had mentioned on Tuesday was that she could only afford the luxury of Shore Haven due to the generosity of her nephew. Now, R. A. found herself at dinner in the company of Elaine once more, and the two were joined by another woman named Cheryl. R. A. made a mental note that she must be the Cheryl the late Mrs. Ralph had befriended.

Cheryl, a onetime beauty with dark hair and hazel eyes, had not aged well. Her classic features had sharpened over the years, and the dark-dyed hair made her look harsh. She immediately took charge of the conversation. After introductions, she tried to pry as much personal information out of R. A. as possible. The latter gave little away and turned it around. So she learned that Cheryl called herself a "people person," had been staying at the facility for three years and loving it, was part of the theater enthusiasts who went to see plays and musicals as a group, read mystery novels, and above all enjoyed a good game of bridge.

R. A. said, "You remind me of my friend Marlene Talbert. Any relation, by chance?"

"No, sorry to disappoint. My last name is Riddle."

Huber told herself, two down and many more to go. Aloud she said, "You have a Doppelgänger, then."

Cheryl turned to Elaine and said, "Is Todd better?"

"Much better, he's planning to entertain us on Saturday afternoon."

Facing R.A. again, Cheryl explained, "Todd is Elaine's nephew. He does magic tricks and was supposed to perform for us last month, but his show had to be postponed when he came down with a nasty cold. You'll love him. He's not only an accomplished magician, but a real nice young man."

"You know him?"

"Oh yes. He comes to visit his aunt often and is practically a fixture around here. Isn't he, Elaine?"

Elaine, who had been steadily eating as the other talked, nodded while swallowing a piece of chicken.

R. A. remarked, "How exciting to have a professional magician in the family."

Elaine corrected, "Oh, magic is his hobby. Todd's career is in investments."

Jim and Jane passed by their table, acknowledging R. A. with a beam. As soon as they were out of earshot, Cheryl rolled her eyes and moved closer to Elaine, hissing, "Did you notice?"

"What?"

"Looks like Jane had another facelift!"

Huber mused, Cheryl may think of herself as a people person, but in truth is nothing short of a gossip.

Over dessert, Elaine posed her very first question, "Are you both coming to Bingo tonight?"

Cheryl said, "No. I'm bored with Bingo; I never win. Besides, I'm in the middle of reading a mystery, a real page turner."

"I'm passing too," said R. A. "I haven't finished unpacking."

That was a white lie. Yesterday, she had finished putting her studio in order an hour after arriving at Shore Haven. She had another reason for skipping Bingo. Years ago, she played it with her friend Peggy at some church. She still remembered having annoyed people with her and Peggy's chatter. Bingo players kept silent, paying keen attention to the letters and numbers called out, in order not to miss marking any on their cards. In other words, there was no way she would have an opportunity to grill anyone while playing the game.

CHAPTER 8

In her room, R. A. settled in for the first phone pow-wow with Andi.

The young woman picked up on the second ring and said, "How's the undercover sleuthing coming along, Mrs. Huber - - I mean Auntie?"

"So far, I've met Dr. Wang, who comes every Wednesday; Emilia Munoz, the maintenance director; and Hailey Sparks, the activity coordinator. I've also mingled with a few residents but have not learned anything suspicious," and she described each person and related the conversations she'd had.

Andi heard her out and then commented, "As I suspected when we met him shooting pool, Tom seems to be a dirty old man."

"I think he's harmless, but you're right. I found his attempt at sweet-talking me annoying. He is good-looking though, and has captured the attention of most ladies in this place."

"What's that activity coordinator like?"

"Enthusiastic, chipper, and theatrical. She appears to be 'on stage' most of the time."

Andi said, "So you've already tackled Mrs. Ralph's friend Cheryl. Did you get her talkin' about her late buddy?"

"I had no opportunity to do so. Remember, I did not have her to myself. Elaine was there too."

"Gotcha."

Huber said, "I did manage to conjure up a couple of last names," and she gave her Jim and Jane's as well as Cheryl's.

"That reminds me, I've done background checks on the three people you mentioned yesterday. Here is the info:

"Dave Beaulieu, age 43. French Canadian; immigrated to the US 15 years ago. No criminal record in the US. There was a domestic-violence incident back in Canada, but no charges were pressed. Has a master's degree in social science from the Université de Montréal. Divorced, no children. Has been executive director at Shore Haven for four years."

Huber asked, "About that domestic-violence incident, did he threaten or harm his ex-wife?"

"I used several sources, but the info on that isn't clear. It looks to me like it went the other way around."

"I've lost you."

"*She* attacked *him*."

"Oh!"

"He was in his twenties then and still in Canada. The divorce followed and he never remarried." Andi snickered and added, "The guy must be shell shocked."

She continued with narrating the data on the next two people:

"Bea Guinto, age 33. Born in the Philippines, licensed vocational nurse. Graduated from Pasadena City College in vocational nursing. No criminal record. Married, two children. Has been working at Shore Haven for three years.

"Caitlyn Novark, age 21. Native of California. Graduated from high school, then took an online administrative assistant training course. Hung out at a party in high school where police were called because of rowdiness and all kids were arrested. Single. Has been working at Shore Haven for almost two years."

Then she said, "Doing the background checks on the new people you just gave me may take longer. I'm also working on another case at the moment."

"No problem, I've got the feeling I'll be here for some time. Since I have no clue what exactly I'm investigating at Shore Haven, I've been concentrating on Mrs. Ralph. The more I think about her drowning, the less sense it makes."

"Meaning?"

"First off, if we hypothetically accept that it was a homicide, the murderer could hardly have been a resident or staff member of Shore Haven. There is a security video camera at the door leading to the beach. After doing the dirty deed, the villain would have been spotted by the camera either wearing wet clothes or a bathing suit when getting back into the building. He couldn't have drowned the victim without getting wet. I am positive that the police scrutinized that video after the drowning incident. If it was an outsider - - say, someone with an old grudge against Mrs. Ralph - - the two would have had to arrange for a rendezvous by the ocean, which is farfetched. And I won't even consider the idea that Mrs. Ralph was killed by some perverted stranger, getting a kick out of drowning old ladies."

"I hear ya," said Andi.

"And then there is her bathing suit, which defies all logic."

"You mean, because her son said she didn't own one?"

"No, I wasn't thinking along those lines. She could have bought herself a swimsuit without her son's knowledge. Think about it, Andi! She was wearing a bathing suit when she washed up at the pier. I don't accept the concept that the murderer dressed her in it after he killed her. That would be too bizarre."

"Of course!" Andi burst out, "she must have planned to go swimming."

"Maybe not actually swimming, since she did not know how, but at least wade in the water. That she planned to lay out to get a tan was unlikely toward evening in the month of March."

"Could it have been suicide?"

"I doubt that. Why bother putting on a bathing suit? If she wanted to end her life in that fashion, she could have walked into the ocean fully clothed."

"So are you sayin' that it was an accident after all, and that the police are correct in assuming she had forgotten how to swim?"

Huber stated, "No, I don't buy that. She was at the beginning stage of Alzheimer's and afraid of going into deep water. The only way I see it as having been an accident is that she waded in the shallow edge of the water, for some reason got a bit further out, lost her footing when a wave rolled along, panicked, and was then dragged farther out to sea."

"I reckon that's believable."

"Not really. As I said, none of it makes sense."

Before they ended the call, Andi inquired, "How do you like your accommodation?"

"Can't complain. The mattress is firm, the food is good, and my knitting is coming along nicely."

Huber stepped out onto her balcony and looked down to the ocean. Dusk had turned to night, but she could still see the whitecaps on the surf and hear its soothing, steady sound with each wave rolling to shore. When the thought of Mrs. Ralph started to creep back into her mind, she told herself, *no more of that tonight,* and went back inside.

She reached for her phone and pushed "home."

"Hi Peter, it's me."

"I know it's you!"

"Are you still mad at me?"

"A little, but I'm getting over it. The house is empty without you."

"I miss you too! Good night, Peter."

"Good night, Regula."

CHAPTER 9

At home, Thursday mornings were one of the days R. A. played racquetball. On this Thursday at Shore Haven, she yearned for physical activity, so she donned workout clothes and headed for the gym. She was not alone in seeking exercise. Most of the equipment was being used, like treadmills, rowers, and climbers. She found an empty stationary bicycle against the far wall. This would be her first time riding an exercise bicycle, and it looked easy. The monitor showed some time left on the bike, so she hopped on it, inserted her feet into the pedals' toe clips, and started pedaling. To her surprise, the task was harder than she'd expected.

Bill, whom she had met the other day shooting pool with Tom, worked out on the bike next to her. He seemed to take it seriously, judging by the dark spots of sweat visible on his shirt.

He glanced her way and said, "A six-foot guy just vacated your machine."

R. A. had no idea why he shared that with her and smiled at him, then returned her attention back to the bicycle.

"You need to adjust the seat position for your height and a few other things before you can start."

"Oh, how stupid of me."

He instructed her on how to make the seat adjustment and also explained that she could modify the difficulty of her workout in two ways. Number one, she could control the resistance on the flywheel attached to the pedals by operating a lever. Number two, she could change the cadence, meaning the speed at which the pedals turned. Bill continued to educate her on all the bicycle's functions, never missing a beat with his own training session.

R. A. set everything at a median difficulty level and went to work. After about 20 minutes of intensive pedaling, she got winded, having reached the limit of her cardiovascular endurance. She backed off and lowered her pace to walking speed while looking around the gym. Some of the other machines were available now, but she was no longer in the mood for trying them out. Instead, she took a few sips of her bottled water and then went at it for several more minutes but was basically bored with the activity. Riding a stationary bicycle could never compare with the thrill of competing against an opponent in a one-on-one sport.

Ready to leave, R. A. thanked Bill for his help, who waved her off with a "no problem" gesture.

She went back to her studio to shower and change. The weather had turned 10 degrees colder since the previous day. At dawn, she had watched the fog rolling in from her window, and now it didn't look like it was going to lift anytime soon. She chose to wear a long, black-and-silver sweater over black leggings. It was mid-morning when she decided to take advantage of the pleasant Tiki Bar and sat down at a small table. She was sipping hot tea when Bill showed up.

"May I join you?" he asked.

"Please do."

After he got his coffee, she asked, "How long do you usually work out?"

"I try to get at least an hour in every day."

"That's true dedication," R. A. remarked.

"Keeping fit is my only gratification left in life."

She didn't respond, just looked at him expectantly, sensing that the man was about to pour his heart out.

Sure enough, after a moment of silence he said, "I've turned 80 a couple of weeks ago. Since I've lost my wife, nothing seems worthwhile any longer. We used to do everything together. Traveling, skiing, mountain climbing, canyoneering, sailing, you name it. There wasn't a thing my woman shied away from. When she passed, I couldn't stand living in our house alone, where everything reminded me of her. So I sold it and moved here. The place is nice; good food and plenty to do, with the big bonus of beach access, where I can take a dip in the ocean anytime I please. Still, I can't shake the memory of what my life used to be."

"I understand," R. A. said, "I'm without my husband too," hoping the sadness in her voice rang true.

"The kids are trying, but it's not the same."

"Exactly. They have their own lives to live."

Bill suddenly was embarrassed and professed, "I usually don't dump on people. Don't know what came over me."

He quickly finished his coffee and was in a hurry to leave the Tiki Bar.

CHAPTER 10

In the afternoon, R. A. sat on her favorite couch in the lounge with her knitting visibly growing. Rose walked in, and as she passed by, gave R. A. a dirty look, then made a point of choosing a lounge chair clear across the room, as far away from the other as possible. Before R. A. could dwell on what changed Rose's attitude toward her, there was a disturbance in the lounge.

Two assisted-resident men - - both well into their eighties, accompanied by a caregiver - - shuffled in, and one of them shouted at the top of his lungs, "I don't want to play any games!"

Patiently, the African-American certified nursing assistant said, "Charley, I know you had your heart set on walking at the beach today, but the weather has turned nasty. It's even raining right now."

Charley argued, "A little drizzle doesn't hurt anyone," but he had calmed down and meekly followed her to a game table.

The caregiver got the two men interested in a board game, so peace and harmony were restored in the lounge. She then walked over to chat with the new resident, introducing herself as Minerva Moore.

She remarked, "I'm pleased to see you're being productive." And having an idea, she added, "I bet there are other residents interested in knitting. I'm going to mention it to Hailey, our activity coordinator. Maybe she'll organize a knitting club."

R. A. said, "I've met her and from what I've observed, she's good at organizing, as well as cheering people on."

Minerva laughed and said, "Like a cheerleader!"

Charley raised his voice again and hollered, "You're cheating!"

"I'm not!"

"Excuse me," Minerva said, hurrying back to where the two men sat.

"He cheated," Charley maintained.

"No, I didn't," the other man said.

Minerva took charge by gently touching Charley's shoulder, saying, "Maybe Kurt doesn't understand the rules of the game. Why don't you teach him?"

A few people had briefly looked up from what they were in the process of doing during Charley's outburst, but most were not concerned. Scenes like these were not uncommon in the lounge.

Moments later, Cheryl made herself comfortable on the sofa next to R. A. and immediately complimented her on what she called the "youthful" outfit. Cheryl's own choice of garb that day was designer jeans and a mauve cashmere sweater.

Cheryl lowered her voice and said, "Some women have no fashion sense. There's no need to dress frumpy as a senior."

"You mean, 'honored citizen.'"

She stared.

R. A. explained, "On a recent trip, the following was written on my train ticket when boarding public transportation in Portland Oregon: *Honored Citizens must show* ID. Instead of a senior, I was elevated to being an honored citizen!"

Cheryl laughed and remarked, "Looks like they've taken political correctness to the next level in that city."

R. A. glanced to the far side of the room and noticed that Rose was leaving. She frowned without realizing it.

Cheryl asked, "Something wrong?"

"Oh, nothing serious. I wonder what I did to offend Rose. We met yesterday and had a lovely exchange, mostly in writing. Today, she's giving me the cold shoulder."

"Did you by chance befriend Tom?"

"I wouldn't call him my friend, but we had a conversation."

Cheryl chuckled and said, "Most of us women at Shore Haven have a crush on Tom, but Rose considers him her sole property. He's one of few people here who know sign language and consequently gives her special attention. She is jealous of anyone showing an interest in him."

"Glad to know it's nothing personal." And she remarked, "Speaking of friends, your friend Elaine appears to be shy."

"Oh, she's not shy, just cautious when meeting new residents. Once she gets to know you, you won't be able to shut her up. You'll see! She loves to sing, by the way. The louder the better, although not always on key. Elaine gets excited simply thinking about karaoke night. I guess she wants to live up to her name." Without taking a breath she continued, "And she adores her nephew, understandably so. He's the nicest young man you can imagine."

"I don't understand what you mean about Elaine's name."

"Oh that. Her last name is Singer."

R. A. thanked her lucky star for that bit of news, and before she could come up with an appropriate comment, her fellow resident said, "That reminds me, I'm going to see *My Fair Lady* with my theater group a week from Friday and got an extra ticket for Elaine, but she's already been to the same production of the musical. The ticket is up for grabs. Would you like to come?"

She did not give the other a chance to respond and exclaimed, "Did you see the woman who just walked in?"

R. A. , having concentrated on starting a new row on her knitting, said, "No."

"I don't want to point, but she sat down at one of the computers. She's wearing a turquoise top."

"Yes?" R. A. replied, glancing in that direction. She saw a well-groomed older lady with silver hair in a blunt chin-length cut. She could not make out any distinct features from that distance, though.

Cheryl leaned closer and whispered, "The woman used to be a movie star. She occupies one of the three-bedroom suites at the top floor and has a chauffeur."

"Who is she?"

"Goes by Claudia, but that's not her name. She's keeping her celebrity status a secret, and believe me, she is going to great lengths to protect her identity."

"But you know her real name?"

Cheryl nodded and said, "I was sworn to secrecy and am not giving it away."

R. A. thought, what utter nonsense! Why bring it up if having promised to keep it hush-hush? Gossip must prevail over decency in Cheryl's law of conduct. Aloud she said, "In that case, I'm not going to pressure you."

There was silence between them for a while. R. A. contemplated how best to approach the other about Mrs. Ralph and was stunned when Cheryl unexpectedly brought up the subject on her own.

She asked, "Do you play bridge, by any chance?"

"Sorry, I've never learned how. Blackjack or poker, yes, but not bridge."

"Too bad. Elaine, Tom, Kitty, and I, used to play on a regular basis, but we've recently lost Kitty."

It was hard for R.A. to think of Mrs. Ralph as Kitty. Playing her part, she asked, "What do you mean by 'lost'?"

"She died."

"Was she terminally ill?"

"No, she drowned in the ocean."

"How tragic! What happened?"

Cheryl promptly told the story that R. A. already knew. She ended with, "I miss Kitty, and not only for playing bridge. She was a kind and gentle soul. And smart too. Being diagnosed with Alzheimer's deeply upset her. Before she came to this community she was a columnist in a Southland paper. Not that she needed the job - - her husband left her plenty of money - - but she loved the work.

"So her drowning was an accident?"

"That's what the police determined."

"But you think differently?"

Cheryl took a deep breath, glanced around the room, and then said in a low voice, "I believe Kitty was murdered."

R. A. looked duly shocked as the other stated, "And what's more, she isn't the first one."

"Have you told your suspicion to the authorities?"

"Of course not. They wouldn't believe me. It's just my gut feeling, and I don't know who the murderer is."

CHAPTER 11

R. A. lingered in the lounge after Cheryl had moved on. Her knitting kept growing as her mind dwelled on the conversation they'd had. The chatty woman had left her with lots of food for thought. She was pulled out of her musing when 97-year-old Betty rolled along in a wheelchair and stopped by her couch.

Introductions made, R. A. said, "I have a paraplegic friend who damaged her spinal cord in a car accident many years ago. She hasn't lost her zest for life and cruises the Seven Seas perched in her wheelchair."

Betty assured her, "Oh, I'm not paralyzed and can walk fine. I use these wheels for convenience, whenever the arthritis in my knee acts up. Just wait until you're in your nineties and your joints hurt too." She showed a grin of stained teeth and said, "I'm the oldest resident by far. I've outlasted three husbands and two kids, and may live to see my hundredth birthday."

"Well, I plan to be around to congratulate you," R. A. joked.

Betty locked the brakes on her wheelchair, an indication that she was in no hurry to leave R. A.'s side, and the two had an engaging chat. Shore Haven's location was the primary factor that influenced Betty's decision to become a resident. She had always loved the ocean, enjoyed swimming, and even surfed as a teen. Surfing was in its pioneer stage in those days, especially for women. "Mind you," she said, "that was before wetsuits. You had to be tough to withstand the cold Pacific."

It was hard for R. A. to picture the white-haired, wrinkled old lady as a young girl on a surfboard, toughing it out in the chilly water. Yet, when she looked into the woman's steel-gray eyes, she saw resilience and purpose in her gaze.

Betty suddenly started to reminisce, "Those were the days we did the lindy hop and other swing dancing during the Big Band era. What fun it was! Today's rap and hip-hop music is noise in comparison. The fashion in the thirties was lady-like glamour, and we knew how to accessorize with hats, gloves, and matching shoes and purses."

R. A. was eager to get the talk back to the present and said, "I take it that you've lived here long?"

"An eternity! After my last hubby passed, I came here to die. That was over a decade ago, and as you can see, I'm still ticking."

"You must have seen lots of staff and residents come and go in over 10 years."

"I sure did. Emilia, in charge of housekeeping, and the caregiver Minerva worked here when I first came. All other staff is newer, including Dave Beaulieu. I must say, he is much more efficient than the executive director before him. As for the residents, I've seen a lot of them go."

"You mean people have died?"

"Of course, what else do you expect in a retirement community? There is a steady turnover. I don't think there is a waiting list at the moment; you got a room straight away. Isn't that right?" She did not wait for an answer and went on, "The only unavailable units are the three-bedroom suites, and I happen to occupy one of the two." She chuckled and said, "A couple has been wanting to upgrade their accommodations for a long time - - can't wait for me to kick the bucket - - but I'm planning to survive them both!"

R. A. bent closer to Betty's wheelchair and said, "I heard that there were some unnatural deaths here lately."

"Accidents can happen anywhere."

"Yes, but I understand that there were some suspicious circumstances about the accidents."

There was a sudden sharpness in her tone when Betty said, "Who told you about Kitty's drowning accident?"

When R. A. didn't answer right away, Betty continued, "Never mind. Must have been Cheryl. That woman can't hold her tongue."

"Do you believe what she implied is true?"

"No, I don't. Cheryl reads too much crime fiction; it's making her suspect murder in real life. Don't believe anything she's told you."

"So you think there is no question that the recent drowning of a resident - - I believe her name was Kitty - - was accidental?"

"The police held an investigation, of course, and determined it had been an accident."

R. A. gave her an intensive stare and probed, "And you are satisfied with their findings?"

"Why do you want to know?" Betty asked, full of misgivings.

"For the time being, I'm here on a month-to-month basis. I'm not even moving my own furniture until I know for sure that this is the place for me. If there is a murderer running lose at the community, that fact would certainly help make up my mind in a hurry."

There was a long pause. Then Betty finally said, "You don't have to worry about any killer. I believe Kitty committed suicide."

"Was she suffering from a painful disease?"

"Not at all. But you see, she was diagnosed with Alzheimer's and afraid of being transferred to the assisted resident wing as soon as she got worse."

"Would that have been so bad?"

"To her, yes. She loved her freedom and told me a long time ago, when another of our residents was transferred, that she would rather die than be dependent on caregivers."

R. A. looked over to the computer section of the lounge and noticed that the silver-haired woman in the turquoise top, whom Cheryl said went by the name of Claudia, was leaving. There was something familiar to her gait, but R. A. couldn't place the woman for the moment. It will come to me in time, she thought.

To Betty, she said, "Cheryl hinted that there were other dubious accidents."

"If she referred to Norma falling down a flight of stairs, that's rubbish. Neither Kitty nor Norma had an enemy in the world. The idea that anyone would want to kill them is absurd."

"How did the fall happen?"

"There weren't any eye witnesses, but the outcome of that investigation was that Norma took the stairs instead of the elevator to get from her third-floor apartment down to the dining room for breakfast on that day. She had a fall and lay there for an hour until someone discovered her. She was apparently in horrible pain and only semi-conscious when the paramedics arrived and transported her to the hospital."

She gave R. A. an intent look as she continued, "And here is the reason nobody could have pushed her down those stairs: She was alive and cognizant before dying in the hospital two days later from internal bleeding. Do you understand?"

"Yes, I get it. What you are saying is that she would have told somebody, had she been pushed."

"Exactly!"

There was a sharp edge to her voice as Betty asserted, "Next time Cheryl fills your head with stories of murder and mayhem, tell her she's nuts." And in the same breath she asked, "So what are you knitting?"

The question hit R. A. out of the blue. She had started her knitting project without any thought of creating a real article, but rather used her knitting activity strictly to have a reason for sitting in the lounge and getting into conversations with her fellow residents.

She improvised and said, "It's going to be a scarf."

Betty pointed at the bright-red work in progress and stated, "A bit early to have Christmas on your mind, don't you think?"

CHAPTER 12

In her room on that Thursday evening, R. A. was tempted to log on to her laptop and do background checks on her new persons of interest, but changed her mind. She decided to let Andi do the research because she was good at it. Instead, she stepped out onto her balcony and called her.

"How're ya doin', Mrs. Huber?"

"Right now, I'm taking in the soothing sound of the surf."

"I envy you!"

Then Andi got down to business and rattled off background check results on the names Huber had given her previously:

Dr. Wang: Age 41. Of Chinese origin but born in the US. No criminal record. Studied at USC and continued on to its Keck School of Medicine. (Still paying off the student loan, by the way.) Married, one child. Has been the physician at Shore Haven for two years.

Emilia Munoz: Age 55. Born in Mexico, immigrated to the US 30 years ago. No criminal record. Married, three grown children. Has been at Shore Haven for 14 years; first hired as a domestic employee, then worked her way up to maintenance director.

Hailey Sparks: Age 28. Originally from Michigan. No criminal record. Took some community college courses in her home state but did not graduate. Moved to Southern California six years ago. Took acting classes while waitressing. Single. Has been an activity coordinator at Shore Haven for 18 months.

Jim: Age 72. Native of Southern California. No criminal record. Earned a doctorate degree in engineering at Caltech. Was an entrepreneur; former owner of an electro-mechanics device business. Married, has two grown children. Has been at Shore Haven for two years.

Jane: Age 69. Native of Ohio. Has lived in California for 44 years. Homemaker. No criminal record. Married to Jim, has two grown children. Came to Shore Haven two years ago, together with Jim.

Cheryl: Age 75. Native of California. No criminal record. Bachelor's degree from UCLA in humanities. Became a feminist and was active in the women's movement after her divorce from her first husband. Had several jobs in public relations before retiring. Two divorces; three adult children. Has been at Shore Haven for three years.

"This all seems straightforward. So far, we haven't come across any red flags," Huber remarked.

Andi asked, "Any new folks for me to research?"

"I met Minerva Moore, one of the caregivers, and Elaine's last name sort of dropped into my lap during a chat with Cheryl. It's Singer. I have yet to dig up the surnames of other residents I've talked to."

"You'll find a way, I'm sure. Now, Mrs. Huber, tell me about your day."

Indeed she did, starting with her bicycle workout in the gym next to Bill, and his sharing of confidences later in the Tiki Bar. Then she moved on to Rose giving her the cold shoulder, Charley's temper tantrum in the lounge, the interesting discussion with Cheryl, and finally, the long talk with Betty.

Andi said, "I feel kinda sorry for Bill." And clearly amused, she continued, "Are you planning to set Rose straight about your intentions as to Tom?"

"Yes, at the first opportunity. Rose is observant. I think it would further our investigation should she become my pal."

"So Cheryl thinks that Kitty was murdered and also hinted there were other killings, whereas Betty suspects that the drowning was a suicide and Norma's fall down the stairs an accident. Which one of the two women's opinion is more trustworthy, you think?"

"That's a good question. As I told you before, Cheryl is a gossip and apparently reads a lot of murder mysteries. It's possible that she lets her imagination run wild and puts a sinister spin on any happening. As to Betty, that old gal is a character. She may be the oldest resident here, but let me tell you, she's sharper than most. There's a lot going on in that old brain of hers. During our entire talk, I had the feeling that Betty was thinking, 'Who is this woman, and why is she asking all these questions?' And in the end, she even mocked my knitting project.

"Getting back to their opinions, I don't buy that Kitty committed suicide. Like I mentioned before, why put on a bathing suit when she could have walked into the ocean fully clothed? The whole bathing suit thing is puzzling anyway. Now, in Norma's case, Betty makes sense. The woman was conscious for two days before she died and would have let someone know, had she been pushed down those stairs. I'm determined to uncover more details about Norma's alleged accident."

Andi asked, "What did you mean by Betty mocking your knitting project?"

"The astute old woman saw through me, knowing that I'm not seriously into knitting but use it as justification to sit there, observe the lounge, and get into conversations with people."

"Holy Krewe! What a shrewd old devil. Better watch your step. You don't want to blow your cover."

On that note, they ended the call.

CHAPTER 13

At sunrise on Friday, R. A. looked out her window toward the ocean. Gone was yesterday's fog and drizzle. The promise of a mild and sunny spring day was in the air. A lone figure trekked through the sand toward the sea. From that distance, it was impossible to identify the person other than being a male in swim trunks. He waded into the water, then ducked under the first wave, and was soon swimming farther out. From R. A.'s viewpoint, his head appeared no bigger than a pin above the surface of the ocean.

Curious to know if the swimmer was a resident, R. A. quickly dressed, took the elevator down to the ground floor, and exited the building by the beach access entrance. She slipped a hoodie over her head as she stepped outside. Although sunny, it was still chilly early in the morning.

Looking out to the ocean as she walked along the path that ran parallel with the community's property, she spotted the swimmer, now on his way back toward the shore. She passed a couple of seniors who were out on an early-morning stroll. From the opposite direction, a young woman came jogging, pushing her baby in a buggy. When even with R. A., she lifted her hand in greeting, never slacking the pace. R. A. was reminded of the days she had done this with Sunshine in the baby buggy, many decades ago. Sunshine was the nickname Peter had named their pessimistic daughter, Deborah, who had been a fussy infant. The best way R. A. could lull her to sleep, was by daily "runs" in the baby carriage.

Seeing that young woman and her child made R. A. realize that Shore Haven residents were not the only people enjoying the stretch of beach along the retirement community. Granted, the place was a so-called "beachfront property," but there is no such thing as a private beach. It belongs to the general public. Most likely, the swimmer out there was a stranger with no ties to Shore Haven. Still, she was interested enough to find out, so she sat down on one of the property's benches.

She did not have to wait long before the man stepped ashore and walked across the sand toward her at a fast pace. As he approached, R. A. realized that he was none other than Dave Beaulieu.

He acknowledge her as he got closer with a "Good morning!" but did not slow down. He was already past her bench when she called after him, "Aren't you freezing?"

He turned his head and hollered, "The water is way colder than the air."

She was about to get up when Rose came strolling along the walkway, trying to pass by without a glance in her direction. R. A. quickly grabbed her by the arm and motioned for her to sit down. Rose reluctantly did so. The former got within inches of Rose's face, making sure her lips were being read. Then, speaking slowly and precisely, she said, "I think you got the wrong impression the other day. I am not interested in Tom."

Rose was embarrassed but bowed her head in acceptance.

"Friends?" R. A. asked.

Rose smiled and nodded.

"Do you still want to teach me sign language?"

She nodded again and reached into her pocket, pulling out her little notebook and pen. She wrote the letter "A" and made a fist with her hand, keeping the thumb straight beside it.

R. A. made an identical fist with her own hand, saying, "So that's "A.""

Rose then continued in that fashion: The letter "B" was four fingers held up without the thumb. "C" was forming a "C" with all fingers, like an animal's open mouth. The letter "D" was made by holding up the index finger and forming a circle with the other fingers. "E" was making a fist on top of the thumb. "F" was touching the index finger with the thumb and stretching out the other three fingers, and "G" was placing the index finger and thumb together, like you would grab something.

Before Rose could get to the next letter in the alphabet, R. A. stopped her and said, "I need to practice the letters you've given me so far, otherwise my memory won't keep up."

Rose wrote down, "You can learn the sign language alphabet on the internet. There are several websites with pictures of each hand sign. Or you can watch videos that will teach you on YouTube."

"I'll check it out and then surprise you with my knowledge of sign language next time we meet."

Then she said, "I saw our executive director coming back from a swim in the ocean. He must be hot-blooded."

Rose wrote in her notebook, "The man is used to the cold water. I see him first thing every morning when I take my walks on the beach. Our Dave Beaulieu takes a daily swim in the ocean before he starts work."

"Interesting!"

CHAPTER 14

At breakfast, Jim and Jane talked R. A. into that promised mixed-doubles tennis match. They had already asked Bill, who agreed to be her partner. She made it clear again that her tennis game was rusty and that she had seldom played doubles. She even tried to get out of playing by mentioning that she did not own a tennis racquet. "Not a problem," Jim said, "the community provides rentals." It became obvious that the pair would not take no for an answer. Jim made the reservation, and the four met at the court later in the morning.

Right off the bat, R. A. felt out of place in her racquetball outfit: running shorts and a t-shirt. The guys wore proper tennis shorts and Jane was decked out in a cute tennis skirt. The only appropriate gear were R. A.'s tennis shoes, and she told herself that footwear was all that mattered.

While they stretched and warmed up, Bill informed R. A. of the rules for doubles tennis. He said, "In doubles, we use the outside sidelines, but the service box stays the same as in singles, meaning the serve must land inside the singles sidelines. And as in singles, we serve from behind the baseline and the server has two chances to put the serve into the cross-court service box. I am not going to explain the serving rotation; you'll understand how it works during the match. We play best of three sets, with each set played to six games. They must be won by two, though."

He continued, "The match is doubles, but that doesn't mean we must take turns striking the ball. After the serve and return of serve, either one of us has that option. We need to communicate so we don't go for the same ball. Only one of our racquets can touch the ball, otherwise the point goes to Jane and Jim."

R. A. said, "By communicating, you mean we shout to one another in the heat of the game?"

"That's right," he replied and cracked a rare smile. "We shout, 'Yours!' 'Mine!' 'Go!' 'Stay!' Et cetera."

After warming up, R. A. was allowed some practice serves since she had not played in years. The first two went into the net, followed by some wide and several long serves. When she finally got three consecutive serves into the cross-court service box, Bill said, "You've got it!"

A racquet was spun to determine the serving order, and Jim and Jane's team got first choice. They decided that Jane would serve the first game, and Bill suggested that R. A. should receive on the first point. When returning the serve, she told herself, keep the arm straight when swinging at the ball; little racquetball wrist-smacks won't do here. Miraculously, she returned the serve straight into Jane's body and won the point.

"Excellent return ace with a jamming stroke!" Bill praised, and R. A countered, "Beginner's luck."

Standing in position behind her baseline, Jane announced, "Love /15" and served to Bill, who started a rally. The point was finally won by Jim, getting the score to 15 all. R. A. was the receiver of Jane's next serve, which she returned with an unforced error shot, moving the score to 30/15. The next point was won by Bill with a strong overhead stroke, placed down the middle of no man's land, evening the score to 30 all. Next, Jane double-faulted on her serve, making her lose the point and bringing the score to 30/40, advantage team R. A./Bill. A fierce battle for the next point arose in a long rally, where Bill covered the entire back court and R. A. stayed close to the net, whereas their opponents moved together - - left and right, up and back - - following the ball. In the end, Bill killed it with a backhand smash, and he and R. A. won the first game.

Game two of that set was served by R. A., who double-faulted right away. She got her following serves into the appropriate service boxes, but when her opponents returned the ball right back to her, she used poor judgment and execution by hitting it wide or beyond their baseline. At Love/40, Bill tried to save the game, but it was too late. They lost 15/40.

Jim served the third game, which went to deuce. Then to ad in, back to deuce, to ad out, until he and Jane lost it. The fourth game was served by Bill, and he clearly dominated the court during the entire game, winning 40/Love.

The serving rotation followed in that same order throughout the entire match. The players were compatible, except for R. A., whose tennis skills were inferior, but she gave it a good effort. Bill was the best athlete, no doubt.

They played three sets. Bill and R. A. won the first, 6-2; Jim and Jane won the second, 6-1; and Bill and R. A. took the last set, winning with a tiebreaker, 7-6.

At the end of the match, Bill gave R. A. a high-five and said, "Good job!"

She responded, "We only won because you had my back more often than not!"

Then they rushed over to the other side of the net and shook hands with their opponents. As they walked off the court, Jane giggled and remarked, "Feels like old times again. Right, Bill?"

"Guess so," he mumbled.

And to R A. she explained, "We used to play mixed-doubles on a regular basis until we lost Bill's partner."

"She no longer plays?"

Jane did her nervous giggle and said, "That's an understatement. She passed of a major stroke."

CHAPTER 15

At that exact moment on Friday morning, Andi had another meeting with Kirk Ralph.

As he sat down in the client chair at her office, Andi said, "Thanks for coming," and before she could go on, he asked, "Has Mrs. Huber made any progress in her investigation?"

"Gettin' there. She's chatted with a slew of people already and is feelin' her way in, if you know what I mean."

"Sorry if I sound over anxious. I do understand that it takes time to properly explore the case."

Andi said, "The reason I asked to talk to you today is because R. A. Huber and I believe that the secret about your mama's death lies with your mama. It would help if we knew who her closest friends, as well as her antagonists, had been at Shore Haven. She must have talked of these folks to you."

"Mom was closest to Norma, who was about 10 years her senior. Norma fell down a flight of stairs and later died."

"I'm aware of that. How long ago was that alleged accident?"

"It was in January of this year. Mom took losing her dear friend hard."

Andi queried, "Did your mama suspect foul play?"

"I don't think so."

"But Norma's was one of the suspicious deaths Cheryl hinted at?"

"That's right," replied Kirk.

"Do you happen to know Norma's last name?"

"Yes, I do. We learned it at her funeral." And he gave Andi the late woman's surname.

"There must've been more fatalities before your mama's drowning. I remember you tellin' me that she said people were dropping dead right and left at the retirement community."

"True, she did say that, but we didn't take her seriously at the time. She had a way of making odd statements. It was only when my wife and I talked with Cheryl, after Mom's passing, that we started to suspect foul play."

Andi dug deeper and said, "So who else passed away at Shore Haven a short time before your mama?"

"A man also died in January - - can't remember his name. According to Cheryl, he suffered from all sorts of ailments and died in his sleep. And at the end of last year, a woman - - her name escapes me too - - had a major stroke." He added, "The stroke victim most likely died a natural death."

"Yea, I reckon lots of old folks die of natural causes. So what other friends, besides Norma, did Mrs. Ralph make at Shore Haven?"

Kirk thought about it for a moment and then said, "Mom talked about playing bridge with Cheryl, Elaine, and Tom. She had a crush on Tom, which I thought was cute at her age. I can't think of anyone else off hand. Wait - - she befriended somebody named Charley, who lived in the assisted resident wing. She mentioned that other people found Charley difficult, but she got along fine with the man."

"What about enemies?"

"Mom didn't have enemies."

"But she might have disliked some people." Andi smiled and said, "We all do."

He mulled this over and finally said, "She wasn't a fan of the activity coordinator and said that everything coming out of Hailey Sparks' mouth was sugar coated but all fake. Oh, and she once said that the mute lady gave her the evil eye."

"Rose?"

"Yes, I believe that's the name."

"What about people on the outside? Did she keep in touch with old friends and relatives?"

"Most of her good friends had passed away. That's why she liked living at Shore Haven; she felt less lonely. As for relatives, Carla and I are it. Like I told you before, we don't have any kids, so she didn't have any grandchildren. Dad died six years ago, and her only living sister lives in Chicago. There are some cousins, but Mom lost contact with them a long time ago."

Andi absentmindedly twirled a strand of her unruly auburn hair around her index finger and said, "Is it possible that Mrs. Ralph offended someone in her newspaper column and the person hatched a deep grudge against her?"

"Two years later? That seems farfetched."

"So she quit her columnist job at that time?"

"Yes, approximately two years ago when she moved to Shore Haven."

Andi suddenly remembered an important fact she had overlooked when first taking on the case and asked, "How tall was Kitty Ralph, and how much did she weigh?"

"What a curious question!"

"Maybe, but it's essential to the investigation."

"Mom was a petite woman. She stood 5'1" tall and weighed around 100 pounds."

"I was afraid of that," Andi commented.

He stared at her, perplexed.

"If she was in fact murdered, it wouldn't have taken much strength to overpower her. So the list of suspects is endless."

CHAPTER 16

Exhausted after the match, R. A. felt invigorated and refreshed as she stepped out of her shower. She joined Cheryl and Elaine for lunch, not because she was hungry, but because there was unfinished business to discuss. Elaine subconsciously hummed a popular tune from a musical between bites of her turkey and avocado sandwich. R. A. was no expert, but the notes sounded a bit off to her ear.

Cheryl rolled her eyes at her friend, then turned to R. A. and inquired, "How do you like it here so far?"

"I'm comfortable, the food is tasty, and there is lots of fun stuff to do, much of which I have yet to explore. Most important, I'm meeting interesting people. Besides you and Elaine, I've already chatted with several individuals. I was especially intrigued by a talk I had with Betty."

"Betty is a character, all right."

"She told me that she'd survived three husbands. I wonder whose name she goes by, or maybe she went back to her maiden name."

To R. A.'s surprise, it was Elaine who answered. Interrupting her melody, she stated with conviction, "Betty kept the name of her latest husband; the wealthy one."

Cheryl gazed at R. A. intently and said, "He was Max Scribble."

"The author?"

"None other!"

R. A. took a moment to digest this information before she broached the topic foremost on her mind. She said, "Betty mentioned a woman named Norma recently had a fatal fall down a flight of stairs here at Shore Haven. I'm curious as to how it happened. Do either of you know the details?"

An exchange of glances passed between her lunch companions.

Then Elaine said, "Instead of taking the elevator, Norma chose to use the stairs one morning on her way down to breakfast and fell. Cheryl and I have different ideas as to what actually happened. In my opinion, the authorities' findings make sense. It was an accident, pure and simple. She lost her footing and fell. After all, the woman was in her eighties."

Cheryl retorted, "There's nothing pure and simple about it. Why would she all of a sudden decide to take the stairs, when she'd been riding the elevator up and down for years? If you ask me, someone coaxed her into taking the stairs, and then pushed her down."

"Baloney. You can't force a person to take the stairs instead of the elevator. Besides, what guarantee could a would-be killer have that she wouldn't survive the fall? The idea is preposterous." She glared at her friend and went on, "You have a twisted imagination and suspect murder whenever someone passes, instead of accepting the uncomplicated fact that dying is part of nature."

"What's natural about tumbling down stairs, or drowning, for instance?"

"If you're referring to Kitty, she drowned by accident, and you know it. Stop spreading idiotic rumors. You're making people nervous around here."

The discussion had become heated and voluble, making folks at other tables look their way.

R. A. said, "I'm sorry. I didn't mean to start a war."

Nothing more was said and the three finished eating their sandwiches in awkward silence. R. A. was the first to excuse herself and leave the dining room.

I need to get out of here, she thought, on the elevator ride up to her room. The Shore Haven people are getting to me. She quickly grabbed jacket and purse, rode down to the ground floor again, and signed herself out at the front desk.

Caitlyn Novark asked, "What are you up to on such a beautiful day?"

"Don't know yet. I just need a change of scenery."

"Well, have a great time!"

She took a different elevator down to the underground garage, and when inside her car, programmed the GPS to the nearest mall.

Three hours later, R. A. drove away from the shopping center with bags of several new items in her trunk; a pair of sandals, a bathing suit, a laundry bag, and a Superheroes Legos set. The Legos were a birthday present for her grandson, who would turn nine next month. Not once during her shopping spree did she give a thought to Kitty Ralph, nor the retirement community at large. What a wonderful free and easy feeling! Now, as she pulled into Shore Haven's parking garage, all of it rushed back into her mind.

On the spur of the moment, she decided not to ride the elevator up from the garage, but to climb the stairs leading to the front entrance instead. Before she reached the entryway, a limo drove up, stopped, and its chauffeur walked around the car, then held the passenger door open for Claudia.

She stepped out, saying, "Thank you. See you tomorrow," and briskly walked to the entrance, disappearing from R. A.'s sight. The latter recognized the old movie star by her walk and thought, I know that gait! There is no mistaking it. Having watched all the movies her favorite lead actress ever starred in, she was familiar with the celebrity's carriage. The star had vanished from the limelight in the last decade, so R. A. had presumed she was dead.

In the evening, R. A. called Peter and asked, "What are you doing?"

"Packing my overnight bag."

"Oh, that's right. You're attending the writer's event in Las Vegas. I wish I could come along. Actually, I was hoping we could meet someplace this weekend."

"It'll have to wait until Monday or Tuesday," Peter replied. "Are you making progress with your investigation?"

"I'm working on it, but so far it's all muddled."

"Hurry up and get the case solved; I want you home."

R. A. changed the subject and said, "There is a resident here who goes by the name of Claudia, but she is really a long forgotten celebrity," and she mentioned the star's stage name.

"I thought she died a long time ago. Did you talk to her?"

"Not yet. There was no opportunity. She wants to stay incognito, so I have to be extra careful with my approach."

"Are you sure it's her?"

"I recognized her walk."

"Ah, yes," he said mockingly, "people can't escape your scrutiny by their telling gait." And he remarked, "She was involved in some kind of scandal. Its nature escapes me at the moment."

His spouse brought up another topic and asked, "What can you tell me about Max Scribble?"

"He was a fairly well-read and successful author."

"I know that! Tell me something new."

"He wrote literary fiction. I've read a couple of his works."

"Do you know anything personal about him?"

Peter replied, "Not much. He died many years ago of pancreatic cancer, if I'm not mistaken."

"Anything else?"

"I understand that he suffered a great deal toward the end, and I remember a rumor involving a mercy killing. Why do you want to know?"

"His widow lives at Shore Haven."

"Interesting!"

R. A. said, "Go back to your packing, and good luck in Vegas!"

"Thanks, but I doubt there will be time for any gambling." And he asked, "So what are *you* up to tonight?"

"I'll spend some time with YouTube, getting acquainted with sign language."

"Whatever makes you happy!" he joked, and they ended the call.

CHAPTER 17

Andi took in the tableau of sea and sand unfolding before her. Other than a couple of sailboats drifting in the gentle breeze, the ocean was free of vessels as far as her eyes could see. She closed them and listened to the soothing, rhythmic sound of the waves riding into shore.

"I could get used to this," the young redhead remarked. "It's different from the ocean in New Orleans, and nothing like the bayou, but every time I'm near water, I get homesick."

She was paying her former boss a visit on Saturday, and the two sat out on R. A.'s balcony on that fine morning.

R. A. said, "How about taking care of business first, and then we'll have some fun for the remainder of the day?"

"Sounds like a plan. Let's compare notes." She reached for her iPad and said, "Here is some more background info," and she read:

"*Minerva Moore: Age 53. Native of Southern California. No criminal record. Several speeding tickets over the years. Took a course at Angeles College to become a CNA – certified nursing assistant. Single parent of two grown children. Worked at a Veterans hospital before getting hired at Shore Haven 13 years ago.*

Elaine: Age 67. Native of the Bay area in California. No criminal record. Attended UC Berkeley, but dropped out in her sophomore year to join a hippie commune. Was in a two-year marriage - - no kids. Went back to her maiden name after the divorce and stayed single. Attended a school of cosmetology and then worked as beautician at a high-end salon. Has been at Shore Haven for two and a half years."

Andi continued, "I had another chat with Kirk Ralph and got some new data. Norma - - the one who fell down a flight of stairs - - died this January. Also in January, a man of the community passed away in his sleep. And before them, a woman had a massive stroke. Mr. Ralph didn't know the details and could not come up with either the man or the woman's name. Oh - - but he was able to give me Norma's last name. I ran a background check on her too."

She consulted her iPad again and said, "Here goes:

Norma: Age 83 at time of death. Native of Ohio. Obtained her high school diploma in that state. Followed her husband to Southern California and got married at age 18. No criminal record. Homemaker. Widowed with three grown sons; all living out of state."

She replayed her conversation with Kirk Ralph in her mind and continued, "Norma was Mrs. Ralph's closest friend here. She also befriended an assisted resident named Charley."

R. A. commented, "I know who he is. We didn't exactly meet, but he made himself heard in the lounge the other day."

"As for people who rubbed her the wrong way, Mrs. Ralph did not like the activity coordinator and told her son that Rose gave her the evil eye." Andi laughed and added, "We both know that Rose's rancor might have had something to do with Tom. According to her son, Mrs. Ralph had a crush on him."

"Good work, Andi!"

"And what have you been up to in the last 24 hours?"

R. A. described her previous day, starting with Dave Beaulieu's early-morning dip in the ocean; her sign language session with Rose; the mixed-doubles tennis match; the lunch with Cheryl and Elaine, which led to the discovery that Betty's latest husband had been Max Scribble, and ended in the angry outburst between the two friends; and finally, to getting a look at Claudia and recognizing her as the old time movie star.

Andi paid keen attention and then commented, "So it is Betty Scribble; I'll do a background check on her."

"Apparently, there was a rumor involving a mercy killing of Max Scribble; maybe you can dig something up about that."

Surprised, Andi asked, "Where did you find that info?"

"Nothing complicated. I called Peter," R. A. replied with a smirk.

"Of course! Mr. Huber knows all about fellow authors." Then she said, "Sorry, but the movie star you mentioned doesn't ring a bell with me."

"You're too young; she was famous way before your time! I'd highly recommend watching some of the old movies she starred in, if you get a chance. Her acting is superb."

"Sure thing, Mrs. Huber. In the meantime, I'll do the background check on her also."

"That leaves Bill, Tom, and Rose, I still need to come up with last names. By the way, when you're done with all the background checking, please send me the entire list in an e-mail."

"Yes, ma'am."

Andi looked out to sea and thought, all these background checks don't get us any closer in finding out about Kitty Ralph's drowning.

Aloud she said, "So where do we go from here?"

"I'll try to lure residents into telling me about the deaths of the man and woman who died recently, whose names are still unknown to us. I may also bring up Kitty and Norma's accidents again, but I have to tread carefully. My interest needs to come across as pure gossip, nothing more."

"I hear ya! One of the persons you'll be chatting up may be a murderer, so don't blow your cover." And after a moment's hesitation she said, "I've been meanin' to ask you, "Did you bring your piece?"

R. A replied, "My .25 pistol is tucked away in the studio safe. I doubt that I'll need to use it, but I packed it, just in case." Then she smiled and said, "Enough shop talk. Let's go down to the Tiki Bar for espressos."

As they headed out the studio door, she added, "And remember, we're related. No more of that Mrs. Huber stuff."

"Got it, Auntie!"

CHAPTER 18

In another part of the building, the following conversation took place:

"Is the new resident a candidate for us?" the first person asked.

"I haven't approached her yet," the other replied.

"Why not?"

"She's asking questions."

"What kind of questions?"

"She's interested in the recent deaths."

"Is she a threat, or just nosy?"

"I don't know."

The person in charge ordered, "Don't sound her out yet. Wait, be on the alert, and see what develops. Most likely, the woman is harmless, but we can't take chances at this point. And for the moment, hold off on our other target too. I suggest we keep a low profile for a while until we figure out what the new woman is all about. So play it safe for the time being. I repeat, *don't do anything until I give the go-ahead.*"

"Okay. You're the boss."

In the Tiki Bar, R. A. and Andi sipped their espressos. The place was crowded with residents enjoying a mid-morning beverage.

Andi swallowed her last drop and, gesturing toward the adjacent play room, suggested, "How about shooting some pool, Auntie?"

R. A. was reluctant and admitted, "I wouldn't be much of a challenge."

Tom, who sat on a bar stool behind the two women, barged in, "I'd be happy to shoot pool with you!"

"You're on," Andi said, and walked through the open passage to the play room, Tom in tow. R. A. downed her last sip and followed them.

When they reached the pool table, the two players selected their cue sticks from a stand by the wall.

Tom asked, "8-ball?" as he racked the balls.

"Sure thing, sir."

"Do you want to break?"

"Yes, sir."

Andi placed the cue ball behind the head string, chalked the tip of her stick, and executed a powerful break shot into the triangle of balls, landing one solid ball in a corner pocket and a striped ball in a side pocket. Then she chose the solid 2-ball as her object ball and went for the next shot, indicating the corner pocket near her foot rail, and made the shot. She got three more solid balls into the appropriate pockets, one even with a bank shot, before she scratched. Tom finally got his turn to shoot.

He bowed at her and stated, "You're a wizard at this!"

"Daddy owned a bar in New Orleans' French Quarter."

"So you grew up playing. Makes sense."

Tom was an experienced player in his own right. They were well matched and played three games. Andi won the first, Tom the second, and Andi took the third, which could have gone either way with only the 8-ball left at the end.

R. A. had not been idle during their pool games. When Bill showed up and challenged her to ping pong and foosball, she eagerly accepted.

As the two women left the play room Andi remarked, "Wasn't it great to kick butt in there?"

"I wouldn't know," R. A. replied. "I won the foosball game, but lost both ping pong matches."

CHAPTER 19

It was right after lunch when the investigators strolled along the beach and R. A. said, "You're giving up your entire Saturday to spend it with seniors."

"All in the line of duty," Andi joked.

"Seriously, how are you doing in the romance department these days?"

"I've given up on it."

"Just because you've had a couple of bad experiences, that doesn't justify throwing in the towel."

"A couple of bad experiences! Really, Mrs. Hu - - I mean, Auntie, that's ironic. First, I fell for a guy who turned out to be a murderer, then I got the pants charmed off me by Bo, who ended up having a wife and kid."

"That was some time ago. You need to move on."

Andi stopped her stride and looked her former boss in the eye, saying, "You don't even know about my latest disaster, who was also a two-timin' SOB."

"I'm sorry, Andi."

"Let's face it, I have a talent for pickin' losers."

As Andi's southern drawl became intensified, R. A. tried to soften the sore spot she had touched and said,

"These bad relationships made you stronger. Don't give up. You'll meet the right man, no doubt." She looked at her watch and stated, "Time to head to the lounge. Are you game for a magic show?"

"You betcha!"

Hailey Sparks glanced around the lounge where the maintenance guys had set up a dozen rows of folding chairs in a semi-circle facing a single card table. They had moved all other furniture out of the way.

"That will do nicely," she said in her customary upbeat way. "Thanks, guys!"

Earlier in the day, when she'd asked Elaine's nephew Todd what he needed for staging his illusions, he had simply requested a small table and of course chairs for seating the audience. He had winked at her and added, "I'll bring my own bag of tricks." There was something mesmerizing about Todd, and she admitted to herself that she was attracted to the man. He wasn't even particularly good-looking, with dark hair and brown eyes, but the guy had presence. How old was he? she mused. 30, or maybe close to 40? His age was hard to guess. Hailey was not required to stay for the magic show. Her job was to make sure the lounge was ready, and she could trust the maintenance crew to put the room back in order after the event, but she wanted to watch Todd perform.

She checked the time as the first few people strolled into the lounge. Fifteen minutes to show time, she noted. Taking off her suit-jacket and placing it on one of the front-row chairs to reserve the seat, she thought, if Todd needs an assistant, he'll be sure to pick me over the old hags.

Then she stationed herself at the entrance of the lounge, cheerfully greeting people with comments like "Hi there, welcome to the magic show!" and "Nice to have you!" or "Enjoy!"

R. A. and Andi found a couple of seats in the third row
and soon afterward most of the folding chairs filled up with
spectators. R. A. turned her head to check out the crowd.
Many of the residents she had met were present, as well
as numerous that she had not, among them some younger
people she presumed were guests. A few children were
there, most likely residents' grandkids or great-grandkids.
Cheryl sat immediately behind her.

She tapped R. A. on the shoulder and said, "You're in
for a big treat. Todd is fabulous!"

"You've seen him perform?"

"No, but he's even entertaining off stage. He lights up
this place when he visits. The man's got charisma, you'll
see!"

When Todd made his entrance a couple of minutes
later with a great deal of flair, R. A. understood Cheryl's
remark. The tuxedo he wore fit his lean body to perfection,
accenting the dark hair and olive complexion. He carried
a small black leather case, which he placed on the card
table with exaggerated flamboyance. He reached into his
bag, pulled out a rope, and announced, "Welcome to my
world of magic!" Then he scrutinized his spectators and
remarked, "Like the great Houdini once said, "It's all in
the way one controls the audience."

Andi whispered to R. A., "Did Houdini really say
that?"

"Of course not; I made that up!" Todd hollered, looking
straight at Andi.

"Holy Krewe!" She could not help her outburst.

"No, I don't need a crew. I can read minds all on my
own!"

He addressed the rest of his audience again and said,
"And now to my cut-and-restore rope trick." He cut the
piece of rope with a pair of scissors and then magically, by

the sleight of his hand, joined the two ends together, and voilà, the rope was brought back to one piece.

Todd's next illusion was accomplished with Chinese linking rings. He first passed the rings around to audience members, so that they could make sure the rings were solid metal. Then he linked and unlinked the rings, passing them through each other, and forming chains and other complex patterns and configurations.

Todd waited until the applause died down and then said, "I need help with my next magic act." He pointed at Elaine, seated in the audience, and declared, "I will not ask my aunt, or you may think this is an inside job!"

Hailey was ready to jump out of her front-row chair, but his glance went past her and rested on Andi. "You there - - fiery redhead - - come on over and bring your wallet."

R. A. happened to look in Hailey's direction as the latter watched Andi make her way over to the magician. There was pure hatred in her stare.

Todd asked Andi, "Do you have any cash on you? Any bill will do."

Andi produced a dollar bill, which he asked her to sign with his pen. She wrote her full name on it. The magician then struck a match and set the bill on fire in a showy fashion.

As everyone watched it being destroyed, he turned to Andi and remarked, "Aren't you glad you didn't hand me a twenty!"

Next, he took a lemon out of his case and cut it in half. He pulled the lemon halves apart, and - - there was nothing inside the lemon that wasn't part of the fruit. "Oh no!" he exclaimed, "the trick didn't work."

He looked crushed for a second, then peeked inside his leather case, shook his head and said, "No, there's no other lemon in there. Wait - - someone in this audience is hiding it!"

He looked up and down the rows of spectators and then walked over to where Rose was seated. He reached into the pocket of her cardigan and pulled out her notepad. Making sure she could read his lips, he said, "Sorry, I didn't mean to pry, but it looks like you prefer good old-fashioned pen and paper over an iPad." Then he seemingly reached deeper into her pocket and cried out, "Aha! What do we have here?" and produced another lemon.

He hurried back to Andi, placed the lemon on the card table and cut it in half. This time, when he pulled the halves apart, he found a dollar bill inside. Handing it to Andi, he ordered, "Read what is written in pen on the dollar bill."

She read, "Antoinette LeJeune."

"Is that your name?"

"Yes, sir."

"Is that your handwriting?"

"Yes, sir."

Todd received tremendous applause as Andi went back to her seat.

Next, he performed several card tricks, like the Ambitious Card, where a playing card seems to return to the top of the deck after being placed elsewhere in the deck. And the Four Burglars, where he showed the four Jacks from a deck of cards, calling them burglars, and told a story about them entering a house in different ways. The front door, a window, another window, and the back door, as he placed one of the Jacks on the bottom of the deck, one about two thirds of the way down, one about one third of the way down, and one on top. He then talked about the burglars hearing sirens and running around in panic as he was cutting the deck. Then he spread the cards to show that the four burglars had gathered together in the center of the deck in the commotion, remarking that there is "safety in numbers."

Todd staged several more magic acts, among them the Dove Pan and Sands of the Nile. He brought down the house with each. It was not so much the illusions themselves that made his show so fascinating, but rather his deliverance. The man was a born performer.

When R. A. and Andi walked out of the lounge, they had truly been entertained.

Andi said, "There was no way he could've heard what I whispered to you. How did he know I questioned his remark about Houdini?"

"That was simple," R. A. replied, "he read your lips. On the other hand, some of his magic tricks are not that easily explained."

Then she said, "Let's get something to drink, I'm dying of thirst."

CHAPTER 20

They sat in the Tiki Bar once more, sipping their refreshing beverages; lemonade for R. A. and a strawberry shake for Andi. The two were not alone in the room; the charming little place soon filled up with residents and guests.

Andi asked, "Who was the woman in the tan suit, sittin' in the front row?"

"That would be Hailey Sparks, the activity coordinator."

"She sure darted nasty looks my way. Didn't you tell me that woman was always chipper?"

"I think she wanted to be in the limelight and was jealous of you."

"What limelight? I scribbled my name on a dollar bill, is all. The focus was on our flashy magician."

"True, but I can't think of any other explanation why she would dislike you."

Andi nudged her and said, "Look who's showing up!"

When Elaine and Todd entered the Tiki Bar, the only two seats available were at the investigators' table for four.

"May we join you?" asked Todd, who had exchanged his tuxedo for a pair of khaki pants and a polo shirt.

"Please do," R. A. beckoned.

Once the two were settled and drinking their beverages, Andi said, "You're good! Have you considered doing magic professionally?"

Todd replied, "That would be too much pressure. As long as it's a hobby and not a job, I can truly enjoy doing magic."

Elaine patted his hand and said, "Performing as a magician relaxes him and takes his mind off the daily stress of his job."

"May I ask what you do?" R. A. inquired.

"I own an investment company, which can be a big headache at times."

"Well, it is generous of you to perform for us older folks."

"Not at all, I enjoy it. As a matter of fact, I come visit my aunt often and have met many remarkable people among the residents here. Seniors have so much to offer where life experience comes into play, and are more interesting than young persons in many ways." He turned to Andi and said, "No offense!"

"None taken. As you can see, I'm hangin' out with my auntie here on a Saturday."

Todd addressed R. A. "You're new to Shore Haven, at least, I don't think we've crossed paths before."

"That's right. I moved in Tuesday of this week."

The talk then moved to personal matters concerning R. A., which she tried to dodge without much success. When he asked about her recently deceased husband, she portrayed him as CEO of a major company, not naming the firm, of course. As for children, she shared that she had two, and several grandkids, all currently living out of state. At the earliest opportunity, without being obvious, she managed to get the conversation back to Todd and Elaine. Consequently, she and Andi learned that the man's marriage had ended in a messy divorce, and that he was not keen to ever marry again. The new thing they discovered about Elaine was that Todd, her brother's son, remained her sole living relative.

Later, when R. A. and Andi chatted out on the former's balcony, Andi asked, "How come you dished out lies about Mr. Huber and your kids?"

"You do know that I'm registered here as a widow, right?"

"Sure thing, but why the spiel about Mr. Huber having been a CEO?"

"Think about it, Andi. Had I said that he was an author, then Todd or Elaine would naturally have asked his name. Later, they may have googled him and found out that he's still alive."

"Of course, how stupid of me!"

"A company's CEO was the first thing that came to mind. Don't forget, a late husband of mine needed to be wealthy enough for me to afford this place. As for the kids, Deborah lives in Northern California, so mentioning her as living out of state was a white lie, but I wanted to make it clear that I could not expect my kids or grandkids as visitors anytime soon."

Andi remarked, "Todd seems to like old folks better than people his own age. I wonder why."

"That's a bit strange, but maybe he suffers from deep wounds inflicted by his ex-wife, making him uncomfortable around his peers."

"You're jivin', right?"

"Of course, I am! I have no idea why he likes us old people."

"It's obvious that his aunt adores him. She seemed to be hangin' on his every word."

"Yes, I noticed. And what did *you* think of Todd?"

"He puts on a good magic show," Andi replied with a grin.

Before leaving she stated, "By the way, I got Tom's last name while shooting pool."

"How did you manage that?"

"I just asked him."

CHAPTER 21

Bill and R A. happened to share a table at dinner on that Saturday, and Andi's comment about discovering Tom's name, "I just asked him," popped into her mind. How simple and typical of Andi! Now she asked Bill straight out, and to her amazement, he obliged without questioning her request. She made a mental note to do likewise, next time she crossed paths with Rose.

Before turning in, she decided to check the chapel about the schedule of services for the next day. By the entrance to the small house of worship stood a sign which read, "Sunday services, 8:00 a.m. and 10:00 a.m." She peeked inside. There was a lonely woman sitting very still in one of the front pews. Even seeing her from the back, R. A. was almost certain that the woman was Jane, judging by her blonde hair coiffed to perfection.

R. A. decided to say a prayer and made herself comfortable in the last pew. When she was done meditating, Jane hadn't moved and sat like a statue. R. A. opted to wait it out. It was a long wait. When Jane finally got up and walked out of the chapel, R. A. followed her.

She caught up to her by the gardenia shrubs and asked, "Is there anything wrong?"

Perplexed, Jane replied, "No. Why do you ask?"

"Never mind. I thought you might be troubled when I saw you in intent prayer."

She smiled and shared, "I'm a cancer survivor and thank God every day for my blessings: I am alive and cancer free, have a loving husband, no family or financial worries, and am lucky to enjoy my golden years in this wonderful place. I'd say that's a great deal to be thankful for."

She then reverted back to her persona, did her girly giggle and said, "I really enjoyed our tennis match. We have to do it again someday soon."

As they parted, R. A. thought, there is more to this woman than superficial beauty and style.

Once back in her room, she called Peter, who wanted to know how her sleuthing was coming along. She admitted she was "feeling her way" but anticipated a break soon. Then she asked him about the conference in Las Vegas. He sounded all fired up and mentioned being on his way to another event, that very minute. Consequently, they had to cut their talk short, but made a date for Tuesday.

Before hanging up, she said, "If you get a chance to shoot craps, put a five-dollar chip on 11 for me on the come-out roll."

"Noted, Regula, but I doubt that I'll find time to gamble."

Then she turned on her laptop and spent some more time on YouTube, practicing her sign language skills.

CHAPTER 22

Early the next morning, R. A. went to the swimming pool. Might as well make use of the bathing suit I bought, she told herself. The indoor pool was large, not quite Olympic size, but big enough to accommodate eight lanes. When she entered, five people were in the process of swimming laps: three men and two women. The two ladies wore swim caps and were not recognizable at first glance. One of the men was Bill, and R. A. felt sure that the other two were strangers to her.

All were excellent swimmers, R. A. observed, as she stood and watched. One woman suddenly looked R. A.'s way, and she realized that it was Rose. Eager to show off her newly acquired language skills, R. A. signed, "Good morning!" Rose smiled without easing off on her backstroke. R. A. thought, that's a powerful swimmer. So Rose is not as delicate as she looks. The other woman had an especially long, elegant freestyle stroke.

Then Huber walked over to the shallow end of the pool, shed her wrap-around, and descended the few steps into the water. Having pulled up her hair with a rubber band, as not to get it wet, she began swimming the breaststroke in the outermost lane. When she reached about the halfway mark, she noticed the woman with the elegant stroke climbing out of the water at the pool's end. As the lady carefully walked on the tiled floor, wrapped a towel around her wrinkled body, and then slid the swim cap off, R. A. recognized her. There was no mistaking that snow-white hair; it belonged to 97-year-old Betty. Amazing! Previously, she had only seen her in a wheelchair. The woman who had stepped out of the pool was relatively tall and thin, and she had been swimming effortless, like a fish.

Bill, who swam up to R. A. in the next lane, followed her gaze and said, "Isn't she something?"

"I'll say!"

"She held out for six laps! I hope I'll have her stamina at that advanced age, if I'll ever make it that far."

Despite being careful, R. A.'s hair still got partially wet and she had to blow it dry, but made it to the chapel by ten o'clock. The generic service was different from the Sunday Mass R. A. was used to but proved to be a pleasant experience. It started off with the congregation singing a few hymns. Someone sang extremely loud a couple of pews behind her, and she inconspicuously turned her head slightly. As she had presumed, the thunderous singer was Elaine. Then a preacher gave a homily, which was inspiring, but lengthy, and R. A.'s mind started to wander about halfway through.

She dwelled on all the people she had met at Shore Haven. Could one of them be a coldblooded murderer, preying on the old and helpless? But then, except staff members, everybody was old in this place. As for helpless, many of the residents she had met were strong and healthy. And where did the background checks Andi had taken the pain to research lead them? As far as she could tell, they led nowhere. Could it be that the recent deaths at Shore Haven were all accidents, after all? In that case, the suspicions of Kirk and Carla Ralph, together with those of Cheryl, were nothing but their vivid imaginations.

R. A. was jolted out of her reverie when the clergyman ended his sermon and said, "Now, let's bow our heads and pray..."

CHAPTER 23

After taking a long walk on the beach path in the afternoon, R. A. sat on her favorite bench near the community property. A man with a full head of white hair and dark-rimmed glasses was about to pass by with a short nod of "hello" in her direction.

She stopped him, saying, "You're Charley, correct?"

"Who wants to know?"

"I go by R. A. We seem to have shared a mutual friend. Her name was Kitty Ralph."

He stared with a look that was hard to interpret. Was it fear, sadness, anger, or bewilderment?

R. A. said, "Please sit down and have a chat with me."

He looked in all directions, then pulled the hood of his jacket over his head and did as she asked, saying, "I gave 'em the slip, so have to watch out!"

"What do you mean?"

"The caregiver thinks she needs to keep an eye on me. I hate to be treated like a child, so I break lose whenever I can."

"I see." She added, "I met Minerva Moore the other day and thought she was nice."

"Oh, Minerva's okay, but she's not on duty now. There are eight of them altogether, and they work in shifts. Minerva is my favorite, and I like most of the others, but can't stand the one who thinks she's in charge of me today."

Before R. A. got a chance to sound him out, Charley looked at her suspiciously and said, "So Kitty was your friend? I never saw you together with her. Come to think of it, I never laid eyes on you until the other day in the lounge, and Kitty was already dead then."

Oh boy, R. A. thought, who's interviewing whom here? Aloud she said, "I moved here a few days ago, but my friendship with Kitty goes back several years." Before he could question her further, she continued, "Her son said that she befriended someone named Charley at Shore Haven. When Minerva mentioned your name in the lounge, I thought you must be that Charley. What's your last name, by the way?"

He gave it to her without hesitation, and she went on, "I understand that you live in the assisted-resident wing, yet you look robust to me. May I ask what ails you?"

He laughed, embarrassed, and stated, "I'm slowly going off the rocker. Most of the time I'm as sane as the next guy, but there are days when I can't remember shit. Mind you, I can function on my own and don't need any physical help. The trouble is, when I have my memory lapses, I do stupid stuff. I used to have my digs in your building with the independent residents, until I made a complete idiot of myself one fine evening."

R. A. did not say anything, just looked at him expectantly.

Sure enough, he continued, "Ever since they moved me to the assisted-resident wing, they think they need to keep an eye on me, even when I'm perfectly okay most of the time." With a sudden surge of anger and frustration, he shouted, "I used to be a scientist - - a physicist, to be exact - - with a PhD, for crying out loud! I was both a theoretical and experimental physicist and even penned a couple of books on the subject matter. And now, certified nursing assistants tell me what to do!"

"That must be hard for you indeed," R. A. commented.

Just as fast as his temper had flared up, he settled down and became calm again, saying, "Don't get me wrong. Overall, I like it here or I wouldn't stay."

"Do you mind telling me what happened in the independent-resident building?"

He hesitated and then said, "What the hell, I made you curious, so might as well tell you. I ran around naked down the hallway, chasing after a woman. I didn't remember doing so later, but that's beside the point."

After a pause R. A. asked, "Was it Kitty you chased?"

"Certainly not! She was a sweet lady. I wouldn't try to do anything to her, not even on a bad day."

"Sorry, I didn't mean to upset you."

He ignored her comment and went on, "And if you want proof, I transferred to the assisted-resident wing before Kitty came to live here."

They stayed silent for a few moments, while Charley looked out to sea. R. A. followed his gaze and said, "It's sad about Kitty's drowning."

He nodded.

"Do you know Cheryl?"

"I know who she is, but we've never talked."

"Well, Cheryl thinks that Kitty was murdered."

"She's full of hot air!"

"You believe that Kitty had forgotten she couldn't swim and accidentally drowned?"

"Nope. She was over confident of what she'd learned and drowned."

"I don't understand."

"She told me a secret, and I promised I wouldn't tell a soul, but now that she's dead, I guess I no longer need to keep it. She had learning how to swim on her bucket list and told me that she was taking swimming lessons and planned to surprise everyone with her accomplishment."

"Swimming lessons in the ocean?"

"Affirmative."

"Wouldn't it have made more sense to learn how to swim in the pool?"

"That's what I said, but she pointed out that she could hardly keep it a secret, taking lessons in the pool where people swam all day long."

"Did you tell the authorities about this?"

"I was never questioned by them. And anyhow, what difference does it make? They ruled accidental drowning, which is correct."

R. A. was about to ask him whether he knew who Kitty's swim instructor was but never got the chance because his caregiver came along, exclaiming, "Charley! I've been looking all over for you. Are you trying to hide beneath your hoodie? Naughty, naughty! Let's go. It's past time for your medication," and she escorted him toward the community buildings.

Charley looked back, rolling his eyes and said, "See what I mean?"

The lady detective remained on the bench, mulling over what she had learned from Charley. Wow, she thought, that puts Kitty's drowning in a whole different ball game. Someone must have been extremely cunning.

CHAPTER 24

R. A. intended to give the library a perusal and was about to leave the bench when a woman strode toward her on the path. There was no mistaking that gait; she knew it was Claudia, already from a distance. When the lady came even with the bench, R. A. called out her stage name.

She froze, then stared at R. A. in near panic and hissed, "You're mistaken. My name is Claudia."

"Don't worry. Your secret is safe with me."

A couple strolled by, and Claudia, not wanting to attract attention, sat down next to R. A. She uttered, "How did you know? Never mind, I bet it's that horrid Cheryl who can't keep her tongue."

"No, I identified you all on my own."

"But I had my looks changed drastically. How could you tell?"

"I can distinguish people by their walk. Yours is easily recognizable."

"Keep your knowledge to yourself, then." She pinned R. A. with a malicious stare and stated, "Otherwise I'll make life miserable for you."

"I'm not intimidated, but as I said, your secret is safe with me."

"Good!"

R. A. said, "Just out of curiosity, why is staying anonymous so important to you?"

"I want to be left in peace."

"Don't we all?"

"You don't get it! I loved acting, and for most of my life, I wallowed in my profession. What I never felt comfortable with was the hoopla that went with it. I put up with fans wanting autographs and paparazzi chasing me, as well as publicity stunts. After all, that was all part of being a star. When I gave up my acting career almost 20 years ago, I thought I could walk away and be forgotten. Boy, was I mistaken! I moved many times, trying to escape the public eye. But there was always someone: a housekeeper, a gardener, the mailman - - you name it - - who blurted my identity, and there followed harassment of fans. You may call them admirers, but to me, they are persecutors."

She took a deep breath and continued, "And then I came to Shore Haven and found it *was* a true haven. I am known as Claudia and blend in with all the other seniors. I kept my dear old chauffeur, who is loyal and discreet. I'm happy here and plan to live what is left of my life in peace. A few weeks ago, that blabbermouth, Cheryl, figured out my past - - I still don't know how - - and I made her vow secrecy. And now you!"

She shouted that last sentence and darted a nasty look R. A.'s way.

"You'll be Claudia to me, and Claudia only. So you have nothing to fear."

Her expression softened and she said, "Thank you," got up, and walked away.

The library was the size of an average living room and contained four shelves of both fiction and nonfiction books. There was no librarian nor roster for people to check-out books, but a large sign that read: "Please return each book when finished reading. Thank you!" There were some chairs scattered throughout the room, where people could sit and read. When R. A. entered, she noticed Rose sitting in one of them, engrossed in a tale. There were mystery, romance, and science-fiction genres, as well as general literature. The nonfiction section held mostly health-related and senior-living type works. R. A. perused the fiction shelves to see if any of Peter's books had found their way there, but discovered none.

She selected a mystery novel that looked interesting and sauntered over to a chair near Rose, who finally looked up from her read.

"What are you reading?" R. A. asked in sign language, and Rose showed her the cover of the book.

"So you're into romance? Interesting."

Rose signed back, "You've taught yourself my language. I'm impressed!"

Soon they were engaged in a lengthy conversation. When R. A. asked why Rose chose Shore Haven over a community in the deaf culture, the latter explained that she had always felt out of place among her deaf peers, since the majority were born deaf. Rose had lost her hearing at the age of 13 in a car accident that killed her brother and father and left her mother a paraplegic. When Rose got technical about her hearing loss, the signing got too involved for R. A. to follow.

Out came the notepad and pen and Rose wrote, "I had a skull fracture. There was damage to the temporal lobe of the brain, causing the loss of my hearing."

She wrote on, "So you see, I remember what it was like to hear people talk, sing, and shout, or listen to music. And of course, I haven't forgotten other sounds too. The most horrible was the screeching of brakes."

R. A. touched her hand and signed, "I'm sorry."

"It was a long time ago; life went on."

Then R. A. brought the conversation back to the present. Whenever it got too complicated for sign language, they resorted to pen and paper. She first learned Rose's last name and then eased her way into talking about Cheryl's accusations. She gathered that although Rose had personally disliked Kitty, she saw no reason anyone could have had to kill her. When the discussion got to Norma's fall down a flight of stairs, R. A. mentioned that Cheryl questioned the fact that she had decided to take the stairs that morning, when she normally rode down in the elevator. In Cheryl's opinion, someone had coaxed Norma into taking the stairs, and then pushed her down.

"Wrong," Rose signed, "nobody coaxed her nor pushed her. She took the stairs because the elevator was out of order."

"Really? When Cheryl and Elaine discussed the matter, neither mentioned anything about the elevator being out of order."

"They probably didn't know. It was only out of order for a short time."

"Tell me about that morning, please. Nobody shared any details with me."

Rose obliged, and R. A. learned that Norma was an early riser and showed up in the dining room as soon as it opened at 6:30, every morning. Norma's apartment, like Rose's, was on the third floor. On the morning in question, Rose was also ready to ride down to breakfast earlier than usual. There was a sign next to the elevator, stating it was out of order. She had planned to take a walk along the beach after breakfast, so she had decided to get a jacket now to save her climbing the stairs later. Therefore, she had returned to her apartment to get it, changed her shoes, and made a quick pit stop to the bathroom. Minutes later, when she walked down the hallway, the sign next to the elevator was gone and she was able to ride it down.

In Rose's estimation, Norma went to breakfast when the elevator was out of order. Since she was always the first person there, nobody missed her at breakfast, thinking she had already come and gone. Later, when the rest of the residents went down, the elevator was working again, and nobody needed to take the stairs. Consequently, Norma was not found for at least an hour.

Rose finished with, "An hour can be a long time." She shuddered. "I get the willies when I think of her laying there in pain all that time. Tom signed to me that she was close to passing out from agony when Ms. Munoz found her."

"Emilia Munoz, the maintenance director, found her?"

"That's right."

"Was the sign by the elevator handwritten?"

"Yes."

"Do you remember the wording?"

Rose thought about it and then wrote down, "It read, 'Elevator temporarily out of order. Please use stairs.' Why? Do you think something was fishy about the sign?"

"I don't know. Did you tell the authorities that the elevator was out of order?"

"No. They didn't ask me."

The women exchanged a few more comments about the books displayed in the room, then Rose buried her nose back in hers, and R. A. made her exit.

As she stepped out of the library, she thought, I made a few discoveries today. Now it's time to think!

CHAPTER 25

R. A. did her best thinking when on the road, so she went for a ride. When she signed herself out at the front desk, she asked Caitlyn, the receptionist, to please let the kitchen know that she would be absent at dinner.

"No problem," the young woman said. "Where are you off to?"

"Don't know yet."

"You do that a lot."

R. A. stared, uncomprehending.

"Going wherever the mood takes you, I mean."

"That's me," R. A. said, and waved good-bye.

Having no particular destination in mind, she merged onto the 101 freeway. While her eyes paid attention to the road at a steady speed of 70 mph, her mind explored new possibilities about Kitty and Norma's so-called accidents. She first concentrated on old Mrs. Ralph's drowning. What she had learned from Charley about someone having secretly taught her to swim was thought-provoking indeed. And then she focused on Norma's fall. That elevator business was suspicious. Obviously, the killer - - if there was a killer - - wanted her to take the stairs. That still left the "having been pushed" thing unanswered. By the time she reached Santa Barbara, she had an idea and planned to check it out upon her return to Shore Haven.

Meanwhile, she found parking in downtown Santa Barbara and then strolled down State Street. Being a college town, Santa Barbara was bustling with young people on this Sunday, late afternoon. R. A. enjoyed the upbeat atmosphere and having young persons all around her. She took pleasure in window-shopping the many interesting stores and boutiques, and checked out menus posted outside the numerous restaurants. She must have walked a dozen blocks, before turning around and ending up at a seafood place near the pier for dinner. The salmon, served over rice pilaf, was cooked to perfection, and she savored every bite.

Arriving back at the community in Ventura, R. A. ran into Jim and Jane in the parking garage. They walked to the underground elevator together, and she learned that the pair had returned from a day-trip to downtown Los Angeles.

Jim said, "We haven't been there in years. It sure was an enjoyable experience."

His wife added, "The inner city had a facelift in the last few years. The area around Union Station, China Town, Olvera Street, and the cathedral was especially interesting. We walked all over, then stopped for dinner on our drive home, and now I'm bushed."

They signed themselves in at the front desk and then walked over to the independent-residents building.

In the elevator Jim asked, "What floor?"

"Four, please," R. A. said. He pushed the buttons to floors three and four, and then asked, "Did you move your golf stuff yet? We're planning to play a round tomorrow and would be happy to have you join us."

"Thanks, but I'm still without my clubs and shoes."

They said their good-nights as Jim and Jane stepped out on the third floor. R. A. continued riding up to the fourth and thought, why do they want to include me in their golf games so badly? Are they unusually sociable, or do they have some ulterior motive?

R. A. waited until past 9:30 before she pursued her experiment. By that time she hoped most residents would be in bed, or at least in their apartments, and the night-shift staff would be busy elsewhere. She stuck her head out of the studio apartment. All was calm with no one in sight. She quickly made her way down the hallway, past the elevator to the stairway, then descended the flight of stairs to the third floor. She looked in all directions, making sure the coast was clear on that floor also. Stooping down at the topmost step of the stairs leading to the second floor, the lady detective examined the area around that step.

Although there was adequate lighting in the hallway, it did not illuminate the stairwell enough for R. A.'s purpose. She had come prepared, and using her flashlight, crouched on her hands and knees to inspect the wall next to the step. Sure enough, there was a small hole in the wall, possibly made by hammering in a nail. The nail had been removed, but the slight cavity remained. Its location was about five inches higher in the wall than that first step, and R. A. glanced from the hole, across the length of the step, to the stair railing. Nodding to herself, she thought, yes, it definitely could have been done the way I imagined. She turned off her flashlight and swiftly climbed the stairs back up to the fourth floor, where she belonged.

CHAPTER 26

The entire exploration at the stairway had taken less than five minutes, R. A. noted, when she glanced at her watch upon reentering her apartment. She reached for the phone and speed-dialed Andi's number.

"Hey, Andi! I'm not calling too late?"

"Not at all. What's up?"

"I have news, but before I'll forget, here are the last names of Bill, Rose, and Charley," and she spelled them out. "Just asking, like you did with Tom, worked like a charm, by the way!"

"I didn't get a chance to do background checks on the folks whose last names you gave me yesterday."

"I wasn't expecting it; the weekend isn't even over yet."

"So what's the news?"

R. A. stated, "I'm finally making progress with the investigation." And she told what she'd learned from Charley and Rose.

Andi listened carefully and then asked, "So you don't buy Charley's take that Kitty Ralph got over confident after taking lessons and went for a swim in the ocean by herself?"

"Not a chance! In my opinion, someone manipulated her into believing that she would get swimming instructions in the ocean. That person, the killer, took her out to sea and, instead of teaching her to swim, willfully drowned her."

Andi remarked, "That makes more sense than anything else we came up with about Kitty's drowning." She added, "The murderer must have been somebody she trusted. Remember, Kirk Ralph told me that she was afraid of water."

"Yes, the idea of a random killing by a stranger is definitely out."

Andi remarked, "Learning sign language sure paid off; Rose warmed up to you. That was a crucial thing you learned from her about that sign by the elevator. It was phony, of course!"

"I'm sure of it."

"But wait a minute! Didn't we establish that Norma could hardly have been pushed down the stairs, since she could've reported it before dying two days later?"

"Oh, she wasn't pushed," said R. A., and shared the research she had conducted on the stairway, minutes earlier.

There was a pause on the line before Andi said, "I don't get the thing about the nail in the wall. What am I missin'?"

R. A. admitted, "I had to think long and hard about that possibility while driving to Santa Barbara. Then, when I checked the scene of the crime on my hands and knees, it all fit the way I had imagined it."

"Tell me already! I can't take the suspense."

"The murderer wrapped the end of a piece of fishing line or some other similar transparent twine around the nail, stretched it across the top step, and fastened the other end onto the railing."

"Holy Krewe! Norma tripped over the line, making her tumble down the stairs. How did you figure that out?"

"I was thinking that there had to be another explanation for her fall rather than having been pushed. Maybe she stumbled over something? If so, it had to be an object not easily noticed. I came up with the idea of a fishing line being pulled across the topmost step of the flight of stairs, and in the evening, when I found that small hole in the wall about five inches above the step, my theory became reality."

"Way to go, Mrs. Huber!"

"So here is how I picture Norma's murder was done. Obviously, it had been an inside job. The killer knew that Norma was in the habit of riding the elevator down to the ground floor at 6:30 every morning, as soon as the dining room opened for breakfast, and that she was way ahead of everyone else. He or she did the dirty deed at the stairwell a few minutes before 6:30. Hammering a nail into the wall and attaching the fishing line to nail and railing could not have taken more than a couple of minutes. At that hour in the morning, chances were slim that the person would come across any residents or staff members on the stairs. Then the culprit hurried over to the elevator and placed the sign with the fake information next to it."

She continued, "If this person lived on the third floor, keeping the door to his/her apartment ajar while listening for Norma's footsteps would have been easy as pie. If not, there are plenty of places the villain could have hidden in the hallway. As soon as Norma got to the stairs and fell down, all he or she would have had to do is remove the sign by the elevator and then collect the twine and pull the nail from the wall."

Andi said, "Sure thing, you figured it all out."

"There is one flaw in my conclusion, though. On my return drive from Santa Barbara, I mulled over my encounter in the library with Rose once again. According to her, the sign was next to the elevator when she first came walking down the corridor, and it was gone a few minutes later. So I realized that the villain hadn't had a chance to remove it straightaway. Imagine the shock and panic the criminal must have felt upon hearing another door being opened down the hallway. The culprit must have broken into a sweat thinking that the new person on the scene would also take the stairs and either fall down as well, or notice the fishing line, which may have been broken by then. He or she didn't have a choice but to go back to his hiding place and wait it out.

"As we know, luck was on the side of the killer. Rose decided to go back to her apartment, thus giving him time to cover his tracks."

"One thing, though," Andi questioned, "how could our murderer be sure Norma would die?"

"There was no guarantee that she would, but chances were great. Don't forget, the woman was 83 years old. A fall down that long flight of stairs would most likely be fatal. If not right away, she could die of complications later, and the longer she lay unattended, the greater the possibility that she would end up dead. If per chance she would have survived, the killer was not at risk to be found out. Her fall would be recorded as accidental."

Andi said, "So you discovered how it was done in both Kitty and Norma's killings. Now all we need to figure is whodunit!"

R. A. replied, "It would help if we had any clues as to motive. So far, I haven't come up with anything plausible."

"You'll get there, no doubt."

Before they ended the call Andi said, "You're doing an excellent job, Mrs. Huber," and there was mischievous amusement in her voice as she added, "for a pro bono deal."

CHAPTER 27

Early on Monday morning, R. A. headed for the laundry room with a load of dirty clothes. To "live the role," she took her knitting along. Caitlyn Novark was there, a guilty look on her face, as she transferred her clothes from a washing machine into a dryer.

"Hi there," R. A. greeted her. "It's not busy at the front desk this time of day?"

"Oh, my shift doesn't start for another 35 minutes." She gave R. A. an imploring look and said, "I shouldn't do this here. It's supposed to be for residents, but they're redoing the plumbing in the laundry room where I live. Please don't tell Mr. Beaulieu."

"Don't worry, your secret is safe with me. Besides, most of the machines are not in use, so there's no harm in taking advantage."

R. A. threw her dirty clothes into a machine, added liquid detergent, and pushed the button to start the cycle. Then she sat down on the bench next to Caitlyn, who was busy texting. She took her knitting project out of the bag and knitted away.

A couple of residents unknown to R. A. walked in and tended to their laundry, said "hello," then left again.

Caitlyn looked up from her smartphone and said, "You remind me of my grandma."

"I resemble her?"

"No, you don't look anything like her." She gestured toward the red scarf in the works and said, "Grandma always kept her hands busy with knitting or crocheting, all the while keeping a conversation going."

"It's certainly easier than trying to keep one going while texting," R. A. teased.

The young woman laughed, then tucked her phone away, and the two engaged in a nice chat. Caitlyn shared that her grandma had died of congestive heart failure, and R. A. divulged that her own dad had succumbed to that illness. The conversation then turned to the pros and cons of what each felt would be the worst and the best ways to die. They agreed that certain cancers were the most awful and sudden strokes possibly the least painful.

R. A. said, "Of course, dying in our sleep is what we all hope for!"

"Yeah," Caitlyn agreed with a smirk, "let's plan on that."

"I heard that a man recently died in his sleep here at Shore Haven."

"That's right. Fred Boralac did."

R. A. would have liked to continue on that subject but didn't get the chance. Caitlyn's dryer stopped, and the young woman quickly folded her clothes, said, "nice talking with you," and was gone. The former switched her load from the washer to the dryer, and then sat down again, resuming her knitting. She did not remain alone for long. Tom strutted in with his usual swagger, carrying two loads of dirty laundry in his basket, which he dumped into the washers.

"So we meet again," he said, flopping down next to her on the bench. "How do you like Shore Haven so far?"

"There is tons to do. I can't complain of boredom."

"My offer to show you around still stands."

"Thanks, but I have no trouble finding my own way."

"Suit yourself," he said, clearly offended.

R. A. realized that she needed to pacify him if their discussion was going to continue and said, "Sorry, I didn't mean to snub you."

"That's okay. Having recently lost your husband must be hard."

"I understand that one of your bridge partners also passed not long ago."

"Yes, Kitty is gone. I miss her; she was a sweet lady." He seemed to be lost in thought for a moment and then asked, "How did you know about Kitty?"

"Cheryl mentioned it."

"That figures. I bet she also told you that Kitty's drowning was not an accident."

"Correct. And she mentioned other suspicious deaths."

"Don't believe everything Cheryl tells you. That woman has a vivid imagination."

For a while, the only sounds to be heard were the vibrating noise of the washing machines, the humming of the dryer, and the steady clicks of knitting needles. Each followed his and her own train of thought. Tom was reminiscing about the good times he'd had playing bridge with Kitty, Elaine, and Cheryl. Even if they eventually would find a replacement, it just wouldn't be the same. Kitty had been a sharp player, until diagnosed with Alzheimer's. R. A., for her part, mused, how can I bring the next subject up without him questioning my purpose? Full speed ahead, with someone like Tom, might be the best policy.

He nearly jumped when she suddenly said, "What can you tell me about Fred Boralac?"

He recovered fast, saying, "Don't tell me Cheryl thinks he got murdered too."

"She does."

He protested, "Freddy had all sorts of ailments and died of natural causes." And grinning, he added, "Take it from me; good old Freddy left this world a happy man."

"What do you mean?"

"He went the way all men would like to go!"

R. A. said, "I'm starting to get what you're hinting at."

He nodded and said, "Yep! I came home late the night he died and saw his lady friend sneak out of his apartment. At the time, I said to myself, 'Way to go Freddy! Still making use of Viagra in your eighties.' The next morning, when I heard he had died in his sleep, I thought, 'Lucky bastard!'"

"I take it you did not share this with the authorities?"

"Definitely not. I didn't want to embarrass the lady. I'm sure she must have felt bad enough. And what's the harm? His heart stopped beating, whether in his sleep or not quite in his sleep, who cares? The reason I'm telling you is so you can put the idea of foul play out of your mind."

"Is the lady in question a resident of Shore Haven?"

Tom stated, "I don't kiss and tell."

"I think that saying refers to the person who is doing the kissing."

"Whatever!"

R. A. heard someone sing a tune from a popular musical, and when she turned her head, she saw Elaine pouring detergent into the farthest washer. How long had the woman been in the laundry room, she wondered. Could she have overheard part of their conversation?

Tom noticed the newcomer too and said, "Right, Elaine?"

"What?" she asked, seemingly puzzled.

"We don't kiss and tell."

Elaine's face turned a shade darker as she said, "Don't tease me, Tom. R. A. may get the wrong impression."

CHAPTER 28

Later on that Monday morning, R. A. walked north along the waterfront, carrying her flip-flops. The shore was getting more rugged, and larger rocks had replaced the smaller strip of pebbles. She mulled over the piece of news Tom had let drop. Could she believe his story? What would be a different scenario of a woman leaving Fred's apartment the night of his death, other than the obvious reason Tom had suggested?

"Ouch!" she cried out. With her mind elsewhere, she had been careless when clambering over a sharp rock and stubbed her big toe, which soon turned into a bloody mess. She didn't carry a purse, so she had no Band-Aids handy. It was best to head home and take care of it. The idea was to go to her apartment and apply Neosporin and a Band-Aid, but when in the vicinity of Shore Haven, she changed her mind and headed for Bea Guinto's office. It wouldn't hurt to feel the nurse out.

"You banged your toe royally," Ms. Guinto proclaimed, as she first applied disinfectant, then a dressing, cut a piece of gauze to place over the wound, and then wrapped tape around the toe to hold it in place.

R. A. said, "Just a minor inconvenience. No five-inch heels for me anytime soon."

Already during the mental evaluation it had appeared that the nurse had no sense of humor, and her answer now confirmed it. She said in all earnest, "You won't be able to wear closed shoes for a few days, and the flip flops you have on won't do. I recommend a pair of low-heel open-toe sandals."

R. A. probed in her lighthearted manner, "I bet you are used to much more serious injuries or illness around here."

Ms. Guinto nodded.

"You even have to deal with deaths, I imagine."

She nodded again.

This is like pulling teeth, R. A. thought, but didn't give up. She asked, "I'm curious, what is your policy when dealing with terminally ill persons?"

"Depends on the illness. Cancer patients usually transfer to a specialized facility or hospital. There are plenty of other terminal diseases, and those patients are usually referred to hospice and palliative care toward their last few months."

"What if someone dies suddenly from a stroke, heart attack, or accident?"

"Then we call the authorities, who'll take over." She pointed at the injured big toe and said, "Come back tomorrow for a change of dressing," and R. A. felt herself dismissed.

As per nurse's orders, she went to her room after lunch and changed into sandals. She checked her e-mail and saw there was one from Andi with an attachment of the entire background check list. R. A. was glad to have brought her printer along on this undercover job. She now printed out the attachment, which first listed the information on the dozen people Andi had previously researched. Then it itemized the background check list on the rest of the suspects, which read:

New research:

Betty: *Age 97. Native of Southern California. No criminal record. Was on the US Swim Team and participated in the 1936 Summer Olympics in Berlin, Germany. Married three times. Divorced the first husband, stayed married to the other two until their deaths. Her latest spouse was Max Scribble, who passed away 12 years ago. Two children from her second marriage; both passed within the last few years. Has lived at Shore Haven for 11 years.*

About that mercy-killing rumor of Max Scribble: It took some doing, but I found the info: There was an investigation. Betty and a nurse who came in daily to take care of the severely ill man with pancreatic cancer were both under suspicion. The investigation was suddenly dropped. (If you ask me, letting him die was a blessing.)

Claudia: *Age 82. Native of Minnesota. Moved to Southern California after high school to pursue acting. No criminal record. Landed a couple of leading roles in the theater and was then discovered by Hollywood. Starred in numerous movies. Was married twice; divorced her first husband, a fellow actor. Has been widowed for many years since her second husband's death. Has one daughter from her first marriage, who lives in Paris, France. Her second husband, a tycoon, died 19 years ago when his private plane crashed. There was a scandal about that. Apparently, his mistress was on board and also perished. Soon after that, Claudia stepped out of the limelight and has kept a low profile ever since. I could not find a record of her living at Shore Haven, so don't know how long she's been there.*

Tom: *Age 74. Was born in Colorado. Has a DUI record. Graduated from USC with a master's degree in architecture. Was a California licensed architect before his retirement. Married twice; divorced his first wife and lost the second in a speedboat accident. Has two sons living out of state and a daughter in Northern California. Has lived at Shore Haven for two years.*

Bill: Age 80. Native of Southern California. No criminal record. Received a master's degree from California State University, Long Beach in athletic training and obtained a State license. Worked at UC San Diego as athletic trainer for their baseball, basketball, soccer, and tennis teams. In later years, he became a personal trainer for celebrities. Was married and lost his wife to breast cancer. Has two daughters. Has been at Shore Haven for three years.

Rose: Age 73. Native of Arizona. No criminal record. Got her teacher's credential from Arizona State University. Was an elementary school teacher at California School for the Deaf. Lost her hearing in a car accident as a child, which killed her father and brother and left her mother a paraplegic. A drunk driver driving the wrong way caused the accident, triggering a head-on collision. There was a huge settlement for Rose and her mom. Single and has never married. Has lived at Shore Haven for four years.

Charley: Age 85. Native of Southern California. No criminal record. Received his PhD in physics from Stanford University in Palo Alto, California. Obtained a post-doctoral fellowship from the California Institute of Technology in Pasadena. Worked as a physicist in the scientific research and development services industry. Had been married to the same woman for over 50 years. She died of a stroke. Three children, all living in the state of California. Has been at Shore Haven for five years."

R. A. wrote Andi a quick thank-you return e-mail and then took her time to study each entry on the long list, handwriting her comments into the margins. Finally, she had an idea and decided to try it out on Betty.

CHAPTER 29

The best bet was the lounge, where Betty tended to socialize most afternoons. So R. A. stationed herself on 'her spot' on the sofa. Her knitting had grown substantially and looked like it was turning into a Christmas scarf, no doubt.

Hailey Sparks sashayed in with her customary bravado and shouted, "Listen up, everyone! At 3:45 this afternoon we're showing another movie from our nature series. This one is about wildlife in Africa. It is spectacular, and" - - she checked her wristwatch - - "starts in half an hour." Looking all around her, making sure there was an audience, she continued, "Don't forget the dance lessons at 7:00 this evening. I understand that the Tango is on the agenda tonight. And tomorrow afternoon, I'm taking you to play mini golf. So sign up, if you haven't already."

With the aid of a cane, Betty had walked in right behind the activity coordinator, and then got comfortable on the couch next to R. A., who asked, "No wheelchair today?"

"On a sunny day like today, my arthritis is manageable. I wouldn't even need the walking stick, but I guess it's my security blanket."

"And you take to water like a fish! At our last chat, you mentioned enjoying swimming. What an understatement! I got a glimpse of you in the pool the other day."

Betty admitted, "Swimming was my life at one time. Now it's just something I enjoy doing as a daily routine."

"You used to compete?"

"Correct, a long time ago. The 100-meter freestyle was my specialty. It even got me to the 1936 Summer Olympics in Berlin, Germany. I did not bring home any medals, though. At 17, I was not quite strong enough." She stared into space, and not without regret added, "I would have had a better chance in the 1940 Olympics, but they were cancelled due to World War II."

R. A. stated, "Just participating was an honor."

"That's right. I enjoyed every moment, but as I said, it was a long time ago."

R. A. knew she had to tread carefully with her next topic and said, "You told me the other day that you've survived three husbands and two children. Does that mean that you have no more relatives?"

"Correct; my sister passed three years ago. As far as I know, she was my last kin alive."

"Who will inherit your assets?"

"That is hardly any of your business."

Something suddenly occurred to Betty. She stared at R. A. and roared, "You people disgust me! Planting you here, pretending to be a harmless little old knitting lady."

She got up and raised her cane in a menacing gesture, and for a split second R. A. thought that she would strike her with it. Then she lowered it, walked away and out the door, without another glance in R. A.'s direction.

Ms. Sparks and a maintenance employee had set up folding chairs and the lounge was rapidly filling with residents, eager to watch the movie. Plenty of people heard Betty's loud outburst before she stormed off.

Cheryl stepped over to where R. A. sat and asked, "What on earth did you say to Betty that made her so angry?"

"Just a minor misunderstanding. Nothing to worry you."

Cheryl chuckled and said, "I should have warned you. The old gal has a temper! Are you staying for the wildlife film?"

"I have other plans, but you enjoy," R. A. replied, and got up to leave.

On the phone that night, R. A. and Andi had plenty to discuss. R. A. told what she had learned from Tom about Fred Boralac, the man who supposedly died in his sleep, and commented, "Tom may believe differently, but what he thinks was Fred's lady friend may have been his murderess."

"I hear ya! Her purpose for being in his apartment was perhaps not to make love but to kill," Andi said, then followed her train of thought and relayed, "So we can assume that Kitty and Norma were murdered, and if Fred was also bumped off, we're lookin' for a woman as the villain."

"True, unless there is more than one person involved. Listen to what happened during my chat with Betty today, and you'll understand what I mean." She repeated the conversation, word for word.

Andi asked, "What do you think she meant by 'you people'?"

"I thought about that in depth and came up with the following: She must have been approached about leaving her money to someone, or a group of people. Then, when I inquired about beneficiaries of her will, she jumped to the conclusion that I was in cahoots with them."

Andi said, "She most likely told those folks to go pound sand, and when she figured that they sent you to pester her again, she blew her top. What made you ask about her will in the first place?"

"Since I cannot find a common denominator with the victims, I thought that money may play a role, even though you established right off the bat that Kitty Ralph's son inherited the bulk of her assets."

"Got it. But what made you focus on Betty?"

R. A. explained her reasoning. "Maybe with the exception of Elaine, who lives here by the kindness of her nephew, all residents are more or less well to do. Most likely, the wealthiest are Betty and Claudia, and of the two, Betty is easier to talk to."

"So we finally have a motive for the murders, and it is the old, vulgar stink of money."

"Unless I'm wrong, which could be just as likely," R. A. admitted.

They were ready to end the call when she said, "It wouldn't hurt to ask Kirk and Carla Ralph to whom Kitty bestowed those legacies in her will, and what the amounts are."

"Sure thing, Mrs. Huber, I'll contact them. They're anxious to know how the investigation is coming along, and now I can tell them that we're making progress."

"As for Norma and Fred, making an inquiry into who inherited their money may not be as easy a task," said R. A.

CHAPTER 30

On Tuesday, R. A. was to meet Peter at the fish place by the pier for lunch. She decided to leave her car in the garage and walk the short distance. Her right big toe was still a bit of a problem, but with the flat open-toe sandals, she managed.

She started off going south along the bike-and-pedestrian path running parallel with the ocean. When she turned a bend, the pier came into view approximately a mile away. 15 minutes into her walk, the path widened into a pleasant oceanfront promenade. She came upon manmade mini hoodoos, built from rocks, which stood in the sand next to the walkway. Beyond the stone sculptures, a few surfers were riding the waves. She halted her stride to admire the rock creations and watch the surfers.

Soon she passed an apartment complex to her left, and then a 12-story box-shaped hotel, sticking out like a sore thumb amid the flat landscape. The fish restaurant was located at the beginning of the pier, and climbing the stairs leading up to it, she suddenly got a rush of anticipation to see her hubby. Peter was already waiting inside, seated at a window table overlooking the ocean. He got up from his chair as she made her way over.

She rushed into his arms and said, "So good to see you! It's only been a week, but feels like months!"

"I sort of missed you too," he teased.

They each ordered a salmon salad and watched the seagulls fly by close to their window. Out on the pier, a pelican stood perched on a crossbeam, seemingly motionless. He suddenly dove, beak-first, into the water to catch a fish.

"Did you see that?" she cried out.

"I sure did. Unlike us, he works hard for his lunch."

The waitress brought their plates, and they ate in agreeable silence, taking pleasure in the serenity of the setting. It was only over coffee that they started to speak.

R. A. said, "So how was your conference in Las Vegas?"

"Great! The speakers gave excellent presentations. I attended a couple of workshops and learned a thing or two, but most important are the valuable contacts I made." He smiled at her meekly and added, "Sorry, Regula, I didn't get a chance to gamble, so couldn't put your five-dollar bet on 11 at the craps table."

"I haven't heard my name in a week; it's music to my ears!"

"So what's up with the sleuthing?"

"Since you didn't want me to take this undercover assignment in the first place, are you even up to talking shop?"

"Will it help with your coming home sooner?"

"It might."

"Then shoot!"

R. A. kept him up to date with what she had learned from residents and staff members, and described the result of her staircase research. Peter listened carefully to her long tale, without interrupting.

When her narrative came to an end, he whistled and said, "It sounds like triple foul play to me. And the money angle as a motive makes sense. Some ruthless person or persons may have talked these old folks into bequeathing them money, and then killed for it. All you have to do is find out who the beneficiaries in the wills of the three dead people are, and you've solved the case."

"Easy as pie," his wife said sarcastically.

Then she reached into her purse and, handing him the suspects' background list, said, "I brought this along, just in case. The order of names on the list is as Andi researched them and has nothing to do with the priority of suspects."

"Aha!" Peter said, "you knew I'd be easy prey." He took his time studying the long list. Then he focused on the handwritten comments in the margins on each person. They read:

"**Dave Beaulieu:** A great swimmer. **Bea Guinto:** Need to find out what makes her tick. **Caitlyn Novark:** Seems a nice young woman. Is afraid of the executive director. **Dr. Wang:** Have Andi find out from the Ralphs which day of the week Kitty drowned. **Emilia Munoz:** Found Norma after fall on the stairs. **Hailey Sparks:** Isn't always as chipper as she appears. **Minerva Moore:** Is her knack for handling old folks a disguise? **Jim:** Too nice to be true? **Jane:** Has more depth than at first glance. **Cheryl:** Are her accusations a clever cover? **Elaine:** Not as meek as she appears (Heated dispute with Cheryl). **Betty:** Could be one of the wealthiest residents. **Claudia:** Will go to great lengths to avoid having her true identity uncovered, but murder? **Tom:** That's why he no longer drives. **Bill:** Could there be a connection to Claudia? **Rose:** Is not as frail as she looks (Great swimmer). **Charley:** Obviously had a brilliant mind at one time."

Peter said, "Norma is the only person on your list without a comment. How come?"

"My comments reflect either personal observations or what I've discovered about suspects. Norma was a victim

I had never met. The reason Andi did a background check on her was to get an idea of who she was."

Then he remarked, "There are several good swimmers involved. Betty, of course, and then there is Dave Beaulieu, Rose, and Bill. Some of the others may also be, for all we know."

"True, but it may not be important."

"Meaning?"

"Kitty Ralph was a petite woman, weighing about 100 pounds. It would not require a good swimmer to overpower her in the water."

"I beg to differ. If the lady was going to trust someone to give her swimming lessons in the ocean, she'd want to make sure the instructor was good at it."

"I see your point."

"Did you find out what makes the nurse tick?"

"Not by a long shot. She's hard to read. I found her to be a no-nonsense woman, good at her job, but there must be more to her than that."

Then Peter asked, "What makes you think that Betty is one of the richest of the bunch?"

His spouse replied, "She has been renting a three-bedroom suite at Shore Haven for the last 11 years, an indication that she has not squandered Max Scribble's fortune."

"You're right. Scribble died a wealthy man. I forgot for a minute that Betty is his widow." He went on, "I don't understand your comment about Dr. Wang. Why the question about which day of the week Kitty drowned?"

"The doctor is only at the facility on Wednesdays. If old Mrs. Ralph was killed on any other day of the week, we can eliminate Dr. Wang as suspect."

"Unless he met her at the beach on a day he was not scheduled to tend to his patients at Shore Haven."

"That's possible."

"Explain the thing about a connection between Claudia and Bill."

"Oh, that. Bill had been a personal trainer for celebrities, and I thought that Claudia might have hired him as such. I know that sounds farfetched."

"Maybe and maybe not! What about Tom no longer driving?"

"I referred to his DUI record."

"Of course! I should have spotted that," said Peter. Then he pointed to Rose's data on the list and stated, "Now I know why you studied sign language on YouTube. I've got to hand it to you, Regula. When you take on a job, you do it thoroughly."

The restaurant was getting crowded and R. A. kept her fingers crossed that nobody from Shore Haven would show up. She looked out to sea, watching a sailboat glide by, while Peter studied the list once again.

When he looked up from it, she asked, "So? Does anything strike you as important?"

"That boating accident of Tom's second wife might be a red flag." He absentmindedly stroked his chin, a sign that he was mulling things over, and then remarked, "With the exceptions of Emilia Munoz, the maintenance director, the caregiver Minerva Moore, and Betty, who have all been at Shore Haven for longer than a decade, all suspects lived or worked in the community from one and a half to five years."

R. A. said, "Correct. You find that significant?"

"I was hoping to come across one or more persons who were newcomers."

"I see now what you mean. The suspicious deaths all happened recently, so the guilty party must be patient."

"Or extremely clever."

He touched her hand lightly and said, "Sorry that I can't help, but nothing else on the list jumps out at me."

"You've given me food for thought. It always helps to discuss cases with you."

"Make it your last!"

Peter paid the waitress and then asked, "You've got some extra time?"

She smiled and said, "Sure. I didn't expect you to drive all the way to Ventura just for lunch. What do you have in mind?"

He worked his smartphone and then said, "There's a miniature golf place a few miles from here."

"Perfect! Let's go."

CHAPTER 31

Once seated in his car, Peter entered the address into the GPS and drove them out of the parking structure, adjacent to the pier, then headed south on the 101 Freeway. After about five miles, he took the Telephone Road exit. The voice on the GPS instructed him to make a couple of right turns, then a left, and another left landed them at the fun park.

Besides two 18-hole miniature golf courses, the place offered Go-Kart – bumper car – and bumper boat rides, as well as laser tag and arcade games.

They chose course number two, which was the more difficult, according to the young woman tending the ticket booth. The pair thoroughly enjoyed themselves amid whimsical scenery, such as the mystic castle, gold mine, shipwreck, Western theme, and many others. The course obstacles were well-imagined, adding to the challenge of the game. The couple was well matched and equally competitive.

After getting rid of their balls at the 18th hole by trying to place them in the most beneficial cavity, they sat down on a nearby bench, where Peter added up their scores.

R. A. suddenly heard a shrill voice behind her, instructing, "Okay, people! We've all got our clubs and balls. Since there are eight of us, let's split into two groups of four!"

"Oh no!" R. A. whispered. "I know that voice. Maybe I won't get recognized if I don't turn my head." Not a chance! Ms. Sparks had already spotted her and cried out, "Look who's here!"

R. A. had barely time to tell Peter in their Swiss language, "Let me do the talking," before the entire gang headed their way, Cheryl and Elaine among them.

Cheryl inquired, "Are you going to introduce your friend to us?"

R. A. said, "Meet my brother," and introduced him to everyone as Paul.

Cheryl nudged Elaine and said to her friend, "She's been hiding him from us."

The two women then focused on Peter, simultaneously bombarding him with questions. One asked if he'd finished a round of miniature golf, the other wanted to know who had won.

R. A. stated, "Paul is visiting in the US and doesn't speak much English."

To her relief, Ms. Sparks cut in with, "We just got here and need to move on. Nice to have met you!"

And to her group she belted out, "Come on, people, let's play miniature golf."

As the activity coordinator guided her flock toward course number one, Peter finished adding the numbers on the score card, then said, "Well, Regula, it's a tie! How about discovering today's winner at the arcade?"

"Deal," she replied.

They played several turns of skee-ball, leaving Peter with the highest score. Then they engaged in fierce air hockey battles, where R. A. won two out of three. As they left the fun park, she pronounced them both winners.

On the ride back, Peter said, "What possessed you to introduce me as your brother?"

"Sorry, but I'm registered at Shore Haven as widowed."

"I see. Why Paul? You could have at least left me my name."

"No, because on my application form, I listed my dead husband as Peter Huber. Paul was the first name that came to mind." As an afterthought she remarked, "I hope the brother lie doesn't come back to bite me. I could have avoided the whole situation by not going to the mini-golf place to begin with."

"You couldn't have known that a bunch of people from the community chose to be there on the same afternoon."

"That's just it! I did know; Ms. Sparks announced it yesterday, but I forgot."

Peter dropped her off at Shore Haven's front gate. And as they kissed good-bye, she thought, if anyone is watching, they'll gather that I like my brother a great deal.

CHAPTER 32

When R. A. arrived at her apartment, the domestic staff was busy cleaning her room, so she decided to have a cold beverage at the Tiki Bar. Taking the stairs down she almost collided with Emilia Munoz between the second and third floor, who was on her way up.

Surprised, Ms. Munoz asked, "Something wrong with the elevator?"

"Not at all. I like taking the stairs."

"Me too, but most people don't."

"I heard that someone fell down this flight of stairs and died."

"You heard right. That was our resident Norma."

"It was you who found her. Correct?"

"Yes, I did. And since hardly anyone ever takes the stairs, she'd have lain here forever if not for me."

"It must have been a shock for you to discover her."

"You can say that again!"

"Could she talk?"

"She was semi-conscious and moaning in great pain. I called 911 right away and stayed with her until they showed up."

The conversation had run dry, so Ms. Munoz continued her climb up while R. A. stayed on her course down.

In the Tiki Bar, Elaine's nephew Todd kept a group of residents in stitches with his wit. He had finished telling a joke about two sailors and a minister, making his listeners roar with laughter, when R. A. walked in.

He said, "Welcome! All alone today? Where is your Southern Belle with the cowboy boots and leather jacket?"

"Andi has to work."

"Don't we all?" Then his expression changed to one of mock sadness as he said, "Sorry, folks, I forgot for a moment that you're all retired."

The phone in his pocket played an upbeat melody. He took it out, glanced at it, and then said, "I've got to run. My aunt is back from the miniature golf outing." He swallowed the last sip of his beverage, then said in a Southern drawl, "Y'all behave now, ya hear!" and was gone.

A lady R. A. had not previously met got up from the next table, and as she passed by R. A. remarked, "Such a nice young man! He comes at least twice a week to visit Elaine. I wish I had a nephew who was that devoted to me."

R. A. nodded in agreement as she drank her lemonade. Soon, she dwelled in her own world, mulling over her murder investigation. She had accumulated lots of information in a week. Now it was time to sort out the important data from the trivial. She thought back to the discussion with Peter, concerning the suspects' background list. Were any of his comments helpful? She couldn't tell, at least not for the moment. In her mind's eye, she pictured each suspect and replayed talks she'd had with every one of them. She got as far as Minerva Moore on her reflection list, making a mental note that she needed to learn more about the caregiver, when Jim and Jane pulled her out of the thought process.

The pair entered the Tiki Bar with the usual friendly smiles on their faces. Jane asked, "Do you mind if we join you?" as they seated themselves at R. A.'s table. They had come back from a long walk along the beach, telling all about it. The former listened halfheartedly to their tale of finding shells and making sand sculptures, as part of her brain was still in detective mode.

Jim said, "My Jane has an artistic flair; the dog she created from sand looked exactly like the Schnauzer we used to have."

"I still miss our Happy," said Jane, "even though it's been over five years since we had to have her euthanized." And she continued, "I believe in mercy killing for animals and humans alike. Don't you?"

R. A. suddenly paid keen attention to Jane's rambling. And when she realized that the woman was waiting for an answer, she said, "For animals, yes. I'm not sure where I stand on that subject for human beings."

"Well, let me tell you, any pointless suffering, whether human or animal, is cruel and totally unnecessary!"

As Jane became agitated, Jim gently put an arm around her shoulder. To R. A. he said, "Euthanasia is one of Jane's pet peeves." Then he steered their talk to less provocative matters, like tennis and golf.

Somewhere else within the Shore Haven community, two people exchanged words:

The first person said, "R. A. and Betty had a confrontation in the lounge yesterday. A lot of people gathered there to see the movie, so it was loud with lots of chatter. I'm not sure what the two argued about, but I caught the end of it, before Betty stomped off in a fury."

The second individual said, "Get to the point, please!"

"I think R. A. inquired about the old gal's will, and for some reason Betty seems to believe that we've sent her. I'm scared."

"Don't be an idiot; Betty has nothing on us, nor does anyone else. Tell me exactly what you overheard."

"Okay, here goes. R. A. asked, 'Who is the beneficiary of your will,' or something like that. Betty got miffed and replied, 'None of your business.' Then Betty yelled, 'You people disgust me!' And she also said something about R. A. having been planted at Shore Haven and not being a harmless old knitting lady."

"What has that got to do with us?"

"I think she meant us by what she called 'you people.'"

The other said, "You're imagining things! The R. A. woman is obviously nosy and Betty jumped to a wrong conclusion."

"What about the questions R. A. has been asking about the recent accidents?"

"It's possible that she's not who she pretends to be. I may have to look into that. In the meantime, keep your eyes and ears open. And as I told you the other day, our current target is on hold until further notice."

CHAPTER 33

That evening, Andi was the one who called R. A. and greeted her with, "Guess what? I'm going on a trip!"

Before R. A. got a chance to ask where to, Andi went on, "It all came about when talking with Kirk Ralph and asking about the legacies in his mama's will. Like he told me before, he is the main beneficiary, and there are only two legacies. They are both philanthropic in nature. One is to a mission in Africa for $50,000, the other to a medical research outfit called Alzheimer's Research Field, for $80,000."

"That's rather steep where charities are concerned," R. A. commented.

"Listen to this: Mr. Ralph knew about the African mission legacy; it had been mentioned in his mama's will ever since she first drew it years ago. The Alzheimer's Research Field, though, was a surprise. Kitty Ralph had her estate lawyer add it at the end of last year, without her son's knowledge."

"What was Kirk Ralph's take on that?"

"He didn't say, but I'm sure his feelins' must have been hurt."

"I imagine so, but that's not what I meant. Was he suspicious of the addition to the will?"

"Not at all," Andi said, "he thought that it made sense, since she had been diagnosed with Alzheimer's."

"I guess in a way it does. I take it he's not contesting it."

"No, but I think my asking may have brought some doubt to his mind."

R. A. said, "Old Mrs. Ralph died at the beginning of March, and now we're having April 19, so that's roughly seven weeks. I assume the estate is still in probate and nothing has been paid out to the beneficiaries yet?"

"You bet. Kirk Ralph is the executor, and he said it will take time to settle the estate."

Andi continued, full of excitement, "I told him that I'd like to find out about the wills of two other Shore Haven residents who died recently, and that doing it in person would get me the best results. He said that if I thought it would help the investigation, he'd finance the trips. One of Norma's sons lives in Reno, Nevada, and I did some research on Fred and am pretty sure Fred's closest relative, also a son, lives a few miles south of Salt Lake City, Utah. Mr. Ralph offered to pay for airfare to both places. Imagine that! I told him that I'd rather ride my Harley. And since Mr. Ralph had met Norma's son at her funeral, he was kind enough to call the man, informing him of my upcoming visit."

R. A. asked, "So your idea is that you'll find the Alzheimer's Research Field also as beneficiaries in Norma and Fred's wills?"

"You got it!"

"Don't be disappointed if it doesn't pan out that way."

"I'm too thrilled about the trip to consider any disappointment. I've never been to Reno nor the entire state of Utah."

"When are you leaving?"

"Tomorrow mornin', bright and early."

"Ride carefully, come back safely, and keep in touch during the trip."

"Yes, ma'am."

CHAPTER 34

The riding distance from Andi's apartment in Pasadena to Reno, Nevada was 473 miles and would take her close to eight hours, not counting stopping for gas, lunch, and bathroom breaks. Andi woke up early Wednesday morning to thunder and lightning. She decided to wait it out and ride as far as Bishop, as soon as the weather would clear.

By noon, the rain had stopped. Andi waited another half hour before taking off, hoping the roads would soon dry out and no longer be slick. She took the 210 Freeway West, then a short stretch of the I-5, which connected to the CA-14. The sun was shining full force when she merged into the 395 North, the road that stretched all the way to Reno and beyond.

Andi experienced only light traffic and let her mind roam. She was going to play the trip by ear, having made no hotel reservations anywhere. Surely, that would cause no problem at off season. Spring break and Easter were a thing of the past, and no holiday weekend lay ahead. Norma's son expected her on the next day, Thursday. He was a dentist and said to call his office when she got into town, and he'd make time for her. According to a brief phone conversation with Fred's son in Utah, he was available on Sunday afternoon. Except for those two interviews, she was free as a bird the entire week. The trip would take about seven days, she had calculated.

She rolled into Bishop shortly before 5:00 p.m. under sunny skies and a temperature of 68 degrees, checked in at a Best Western, and then went for a brisk walk. One can make a round trip on foot through the town in under an hour's time. For dinner, she opted for Chinese food and dug into her choice of Kung Pao Chicken with gusto.

On Thursday, Andi reached the heart of Reno at 12:30 in the afternoon and booked a room at Harrah's. They didn't even make her wait until the customary 3:00 o'clock hour, letting her move in right away. Her room was spacious, comfortable, and clean, but that didn't mean she was planning to spend much time in it, other than sleeping.

When calling the dentist's practice, she learned that Norma's eldest son could see her right away, during his lunch hour. She got directions, telling the receptionist that she was on her way. Then she freshened up a bit, raced to the parking structure, and hopped on her bike. Having eaten a big breakfast in Bishop, skipping lunch was not a problem. 30 minutes later, she came face to face with the dentist, a man in his late fifties wearing horn-rimmed glasses and stooping slightly. He first wanted to see credentials. Andi showed him her official badge, proof that she was a licensed private investigator.

That settled, he asked, "You're looking into suspicious deaths that occurred at Shore Haven?"

"That's right. We have reason to believe that your mama is one of them."

"You think that Mother didn't fall down a flight of stairs but was pushed?"

"Not exactly." Andi explained R. A.'s theory and the stairwell discovery.

"That's suggestive, I have to admit."

She continued, "We are lookin' into motive and are trying to rule out the money angle. So if you don't mind, I'd appreciate knowing who the beneficiaries of your mama's will are."

"It's a simple, straightforward will. My brothers and I were surprised that Mother even made one. She always said that she didn't see the need for it, since by law her money would be equally divided between us three sons." He shrugged and said, "She ended up having an attorney draw one up anyhow. My brothers and I inherit the bulk of her estate and she left $50,000 to research."

"What is the research organization's name?"

"Battlement of Cancer Institute."

Andi tried hard not to show her disappointment while the dentist added, "Dad lost his life to cancer four years ago, and so it makes sense that she left some money to cancer research."

He looked at his watch and said, "I have a patient waiting. Is there anything else you need to know?"

Andi assured him, "That's all. Thank you kindly."

"Please keep me posted on your investigation."

"Yes, sir."

On the ride back to the hotel, Andi thought, why am I so bummed? Did I truly believe that Norma's will would confirm a legacy to Alzheimer's Research Field? I reckon that would've been too easy. She parked the Harley-Davidson in the Harrah's five-story garage, walked over to the El Dorado, then Circus Circus, and did a little machine gambling in each.

CHAPTER 35

Andi was off to a late start on Friday. After dinner the previous night, she played some Black Jack and then had a streak of luck shooting craps, where she tripled her money while being the shooter. During her long run, she made all other people around the craps table winners and instantly became popular. Her fellow players cheered her on, and the guys standing close by were not stingy with high-fives. Drinks being free for the gambler, she downed two cocktails in her enthusiasm for the game. Consequently, the fiery redhead got to bed late, and not being used to drinking liquor, the glass of wine for dinner, the two cocktails, and the excitement of her winning spree made it hard for her to fall asleep.

Waking up shortly before 11:00, she barely had time to take a shower before needing to check herself out of the hotel. At that point, driving more than 500 miles to Salt Lake City in one day was out of the question. She decided to have a hearty breakfast and then ride as far as she felt like before stopping for the night. She tanked up at the outskirts of Reno, and it was well into the afternoon hours when she finally got on her way.

Driving east on Interstate 80, the speed limit was 75 miles an hour, so she made it as far as Elko, the last town in Nevada before the Utah border. Dusk had already set in, and after finding lodging, Andi ambled three blocks to the Red Lion for dinner. The restaurant was located inside the casino, but she walked through it without a glance at the gaming tables. Andi was determined to keep the money she won in Reno and not give it away again in Elko.

She turned in early and called R. A.

"How're ya doin', Mrs. Huber?"

"Andi! So glad to hear your voice. Where are you?"

"Still in Nevada, in a town called Elko." And she related the talk she had had with Norma's son.

"Don't be discouraged. You still have the interview with Fred's son ahead of you. Maybe you'll find a connection in Utah."

"I sure hope so. How are things at your end?"

R. A. said, "I ran into Dr. Wang on Wednesday. For some reason, I seem to make that young man uncomfortable."

Andi remarked, "The man is 41, if I remember correctly from the background check I made."

"He seems younger, but then, everyone below 50 appears young to me. Anyhow, when I saw him, I remembered that I wanted you to ask Kirk Ralph on which day of the week his mother died. Since you are out of town, I made the call to Mr. Ralph and learned that Kitty Ralph drowned on a Wednesday."

"And Dr. Wang comes to Shore Haven on Wednesdays!"

"Exactly. And if per chance he was Kitty's killer, it would have been smarter of him to sign her up for swimming lessons on a different day of the week."

"I hear ya!"

R. A. continued, "Yesterday morning, I went to the gym in the hope of finding Bill there again. I used the rowing machine next to his, and my arms and legs still feel like jelly. It was worth a bit of muscle aches; I learned that he had been Claudia's personal trainer many years ago. I had to wrestle the information out of him, and he swore me to secrecy. So that makes already three residents who know Claudia's true identity. Keeping her celebrity status under wraps is not easy. I wonder who else knows."

"I've lost you. Who are the three residents?"

"Cheryl, Bill, and me."

"Of course! I didn't count you in."

"I also had a chat with the African-American caregiver, Minerva Moore. That woman is a saint, considering what she often has to deal with, and she does it all with a cheerful and competent attitude. But more to the point, I learned something else about Dr. Wang from her. He practices medicine as a general practitioner in his office in Ventura and is the primary physician of some patients at Shore Haven, but his true interest lies in studying and taking care of people afflicted with senility, dementia, and Alzheimer's. After talking with Minerva, I followed up and googled the doctor. He is listed as a physician of internal medicine, specializing in the field of memory loss."

Andi said, "That gives me stuff to think about when riding to Salt Lake City tomorrow."

"Hold on a second."

"Are you there? Hello! Mrs. Huber?"

"Yes, I'm still on the line. I'm checking the weather forecast in your area, as we speak. There is no rain predicted near Elko nor Salt Lake City in the next few days. Have a good ride!"

CHAPTER 36

Beginning at the Nevada/Utah border, the speed limit was 80, hence Andi's ride to Salt Lake City on Saturday took less than four hours. She arrived mid-afternoon, found lodging in the downtown area, and had plenty of time to ride up to Ogden, a town that she had stumbled on when doing internet research on what to do in the area.

Andi first rode parallel to the Great Salt Lake on her left, which was saltier than seawater, she'd heard. Ogden lay about 30 miles north of Salt Lake City and the landscape on the approach to the town was nothing short of breathtaking. The Wasatch peaks were still snowcapped at that time of year, and they majestically towered over the town. She parked her Harley and set out to explore historic 25th Street on foot.

The place had the feel of an old-time town with lots of character. Andi started in the heart of downtown at Union Station, Ogden's historic train depot, which now housed four separate museums, then ambled along the three blocks of 25th Street, flanked by quaint, old buildings. During the early 20th century, these buildings had been sites for illicit activities, such as gambling, prostitution and narcotic sales. It had been known as "Two-Bit Street."

Now, these buildings housed present-day businesses, which drew tourists and locals alike to the area.

Andi strolled by boutiques and one-of-a-kind shops, antique stores, tattoo parlors, hair salons, a bakery, and a variety of restaurants. She ended up in an Italian eatery, where she relished piping hot stromboli, which served as both her lunch and dinner.

After returning to her hotel in Salt Lake City, she called Fred's son, Walt Boralac, to establish a time for the interview. They settled on 2:00 in the afternoon the next day, Sunday, at his house in Provo, a 45-mile distance from Salt Lake City. Then she took a shower, put on a fresh top, and stepped out to check on the city's nightlife.

Andi stopped by a bar with live country music and got a tad nostalgic as she hoisted herself onto a barstool. The place reminded her of Daddy's bar in New Orleans. If in the mood, Daddy would hop on top of the bar counter and play the fiddle. In her daydream, she now saw him clearly fiddling away.

She was pulled out of her reverie as the bartender asked, "What can I do for you?"

"Can you fix me a Mint Julep?"

"I'll try!" Getting back to her after searching for the uncommon ingredients, he said "So you're from the Big Easy?"

"Yes, sir."

"Been in town long?"

"No, sir. Arrived today and leaving tomorrow."

"Too bad!" he said, giving her an appreciative look-over.

She watched as he combined 8 mint leaves and ½ ounce of Simple Syrup in a chilled fizz glass, added 2 ounces of bourbon and crushed ice. He then set a swizzle stick in the cup and spun it between his hands to mix. He topped the cocktail off with additional crushed ice and garnished it with mint sprigs.

"Voilà, your Mint Julep," he proclaimed, handing it to her with a bow.

She nipped at it and said, "Perfect!" even though she hardly remembered the taste of a Mint Julep. It had been over eight years since Daddy let her try an occasional sip of liquor, when she was under drinking age.

Later into the evening, Andi was on the dance floor, engaged in country line dancing.

She got up early Sunday morning for the complimentary hotel breakfast and then walked to Temple Square for the live broadcast of the Mormon Tabernacle Choir. She followed Mrs. Huber's advice, "Make sure you don't miss the performance of the choir when in Salt Lake. It is a one-of-a-kind experience." It was a memorable experience, for sure. The performance was free, but a lady stood at the entrance to the music hall, checking people's purses. She looked surprised at Andi's getup of jeans and leather jacket, had her open the touring bag, and then looked and felt inside it. Satisfied that all was okay, she smiled at Andi and said, "Welcome to the Mormon Tabernacle!" As she found an empty seat in the already crowded arena, Andi thought, a good thing I left my piece at home!

Listening to the 320-person choir was a treat, and the acoustics in the place were fantastic. One could have heard a pin drop. And what was most astonishing was that the gigantic group of talented singers was all made up of volunteers. Andi was sure that she would not forget the encounter anytime soon.

CHAPTER 37

The ride from Salt Lake City to Provo only took Andi 40 minutes. Walt and his family lived in the Caryhurst area, and since she was early for the interview, she rode around the neighborhood for good measure. Judging by the types of houses and well-kept front yards, the region was upscale.

As she rang the doorbell, furious barking sounded from the backyard, and when she heard a man's voice yelling, "Settle down, Slugger," the barking stopped immediately.

Walt Boralac greeted her at the door, saying, "Come on in, Ms. LeJeune."

"Thank you kindly, and please call me Andi."

Once inside the foyer, he introduced her to his wife, who was ready to go out the door. Mr. and Mrs. Boralac were in their mid-fifties. She was blondish and he had dark eyes and hair, graying at the temples. They both looked like they had come straight from church. The lady clad in a tailored dress, and her husband wore pleated wool trousers and a button-down shirt. If they were surprised at Andi's get-up, they did not show it.

The missus carried a plate with cookies and a purse hung from her shoulders. She said, "Sorry, I'm on my way

too visit a sick friend, but my husband is at your disposal."
She kissed hubby good-bye and was gone.

Andi followed Walt to the den, where he motioned her
to have a seat on the sofa. He said, "I can offer you coffee,
tea, or juice."

"Just water would be great."

While he went to fetch it, she looked the room over.
It was comfortable, sporting a large bookcase full of
hardcover and paperback volumes on the wall to her left.
A large portion of the wall immediately in front of her
was taken up with a big-screen TV. A couple of watercolor
prints hung on the third. There were no knick-knacks
anywhere. Definitely a man's room, Andi thought.

When handing her the water and sitting down in an
upholstered chair facing her, Walt said, "I don't know if
I should be disturbed about talking with you. From the
short phone conversation we had, I take it that there is
a question about my dad's passing. You mentioned
suspicious circumstances. What does that mean?"

Andi told him that she had been hired by Kitty Ralph's
son to look into old Mrs. Ralph's drowning accident and
that her former boss, Mrs. Huber, was living at Shore
Haven undercover. Without going into details, she let the
man know that some of the facts R. A. Huber discovered,
did indeed point to foul play.

"What has that got to do with Dad?" he asked.

"We have reason to believe that also another lady and
your dad did not die of natural causes."

"I see. Do you have a suspect?"

"At the moment, everyone at Shore Haven, staff and
residents alike, are suspects." Andi stated.

"We saw Dad at Christmas time and he was his usual
self, not afraid of anyone. I'm sure he would have told us
if he felt threatened in any way."

"I reckon he was unaware of the danger."

Walt was preoccupied with his own thoughts and said, more to himself, it seemed, "Dad had a bad heart and was diabetic. In January, when we received the news that he passed away in his sleep, although saddened by his leaving us, we were happy for him and felt it was a nice way to go."

He suddenly stared at Andi and cried out, "And now you tell me that he may have been murdered!"

"I'm sorry, sir, but it looks that way."

"If that's true, you don't seem to know who took his life, or for what reason. So why are you here?"

Andi said, "We think that there is a connection between the three killings and that the motive is money related. It would help to know the beneficiaries of your father's will."

He could not hide his anger as he stated, "The main beneficiaries are my sister and I, and we certainly did not kill Dad!"

"I'm implying nothin' of the kind. The idea is that there may be legacies, other than family, mentioned in the will."

He calmed down and said, "There's only one. He left $75,000 to an animal rescue outfit."

"What's the name?"

"Let me think. Something about critters - - oh yes, I remember it now. The name is God's Critters Foundation."

"Did that legacy in the will surprise you?"

"No, it didn't. My father was a great animal lover; so it makes sense that he wanted to leave some money to the cause, even though I had never heard of that particular foundation before."

A young man stuck his head in the door and started to say, "Hey Dad - - - oh sorry! I didn't realize we have company." And looking at Andi, he asked, "You're not the private eye, or are you?"

Walt said, "Yes, she is. Her name is Andi, and we're almost done." And to her, "This is my son, Steve."

As they shook hands, Andi looked into a pair of blue eyes, then took in his straight, narrow nose, curly mop of dark hair, and engaging smile.

Steve asked, "Is that your Harley-Davidson parked on the driveway?"

"You betcha."

"It's a beauty!"

The elder Boralac said, "Anything else you need to know?"

"Just a couple more questions. Did your dad mention anyone he was friends with at Shore Haven?"

"He liked to play chess with a man named Tom. Other than that, I can't remember him pointing out anyone in particular."

"Did he befriend any of the ladies?"

"I'm sure he did, but I can't recall any name. My wife is better at remembering names."

Andi handed him her business card and said, "If you or Mrs. Boralac recall any friends of your dad's, or enemies for that matter, please give me a jingle."

He nodded. "And what's the other question you have?"

"Oh, just wonderin' how life is treatin' you in this here Provo?"

He laughed and replied, "We like it here a lot. Up until 15 years ago, we lived in Southern California, and I worked in the Silicon Valley, as a matter of fact. Moving here to start my own Software Technology Company was the right decision. It's doing well, and there's no long, hectic commute; I can get to my place of business in 10 minutes. My wife and Steve have adjusted well to the more easy-going atmosphere too."

"Good for y'all!"

She thanked him and got up to leave.

Steve followed her outside and admired her Harley. He repeated, "It sure is a beauty! What is it exactly?"

"This here is my 1990 FXR Super Glide," she stated with pride.

Steve said, "I can tell you're taking good care of it." Then he asked, "Are you lodging in Provo?"

"I'm headin' another 200 miles south to Panguitch today and plan to get a look at some hoodoos in Bryce Canyon tomorrow."

"Do you have a reservation?"

"Nope."

Steve frowned and said, "By the time you'll get down there, it'll be going on six o'clock. You may not find lodging." He pulled out his smartphone and while dialing explained, "A buddy of mine runs a motel in Panguitch, let's check with him."

"Hey, old man! It's Steve," he said into the phone. "A friend of mine needs a room for tonight. Can you accommodate her?" He turned to Andi. "Queen bed okay?" She nodded. "Yeah, queen's fine. Her name is Andi." He gave Andi a thumbs-up gesture. "Okay, thanks," he said to the person on the line before ending the call.

To Andi he stated "You're all set," and gave her the name and address of the motel.

Grinning, she said, "Good to have connections. I thank you!"

She donned her helmet, swung one long leg over the saddle, kicked the kickstand up, hit the starter button and put her Harley into gear. Then she waved to him as she rode off.

Both had felt a strong attraction to one another. As Steve stepped back into the house, he thought, I need to find a way to see her again. And as Andi rode southbound on Interstate 15, she mused, a good thing I'll never see him again. I can't afford another painful relationship.

CHAPTER 38

Panguitch was an insignificant town a few miles' drive from Bryce Canyon National Park. Other than several motels accommodating tourists who preferred less expensive lodging than inside the National Park, a few shops and restaurants, nothing much was happening in the place. Andi arrived at around six o'clock and, since she was expected, only had to show her credit card and I.D. and was given a key to a room without frills but clean and comfortable. The motel parking lot was full, so she appreciated Steve's reservation.

The town wasn't a place jumping with activity, which suited Andi fine. She strolled to a nearby restaurant for dinner and, back at her place of lodging, threw a small load of clothes into a washing machine at their coin laundry. Before settling in for the night, she called Mrs. Huber, keeping her up to date on her progress, or rather on the lack of her progress.

The latter said, "Don't be discouraged. For all we know, there may be a connection we haven't figured out yet."

"I don't follow."

"On the surface, these philanthropic organizations sound miles apart, but they may be linked."

"Get out o' here, Mrs. Huber! How do ya link *Alzheimer's Research Field - - Battlement for Cancer Institute - -* and - - *God's Critters Foundation?*"

"Sounds crazy, I know, but is worth looking into."

Andi said, "What's happenin' in Ventura?"

"Nothing much, but I think my room has been searched. The domestic staff would certainly not clean rooms on a Sunday, but I think someone was in my studio this morning while I had breakfast. Nothing was taken, and maybe I'm imagining things, but a couple of my items were slightly out of order."

"You mean, somebody broke in?"

"No, if there *was* someone here - - and I'm not even sure if that's the case - - he or she had a key, or picked the lock."

"What do you think the person was lookin' for?"

"I can't imagine. My password is extremely secure, so there was no way anyone could get into my laptop, and my pistol and wallet were locked up in the safe. That's the first thing I checked, by the way."

"Could you have blown your cover?" asked Andi, with concern.

"That's always a possibility, but I can't see how."

"Be mighty careful, boss! I mean - - Mrs. Huber."

Andi was about to turn off the light when her phone rang. She did not recognize the number and was going to ignore it, thinking it must be a telemarketer, but changed her mind and took the call.

"Hello, Andi! It's Steve."

"Hi there! How did you get my number?"

"I borrowed the business card you gave Dad."

"So what's up?"

"I have a day off from work tomorrow. How about you and I doing some dirt bike riding?"

"What do ya have in mind?"

"The Casto Canyon Trail is near Panguitch. You mentioned that you'd like to see hoodoos. You don't need to go to Bryce Canyon for that; there are hoodoos to see from the trail. I could head your way early tomorrow morning, and we'll take it from there."

"Sounds great, but I'm afraid it's not goin' to happen. I need to ride my Harley back to L. A. and can't afford it gettin' roughed up on some dirt bike ride."

"Oh, I wasn't going to suggest that you take the 1990 FXR Super Glide. I'll bring an extra dirt bike."

"Say what?"

"Dirt bike riding is my hobby. I have two bikes and I'd drive them both down in my pickup truck tomorrow. So how about it?"

"I'll think on it," said Andi.

They eased into chatting, and it led to the longest phone conversation Andi had ever had. Among other things, she learned that Steve had earned a bachelor's degree in journalism, then did an internship at a small broadcasting station, and now was the news anchor of a local television station. He was 28 years old, an only child, and still lived with his folks. He mentioned that if his parents had not made the move to Utah, he most likely would never have been introduced to dirt bike riding and would have missed out on the thrilling activity. Andi, for her part, told him about her upbringing by Daddy in New Orleans and her passion for riding the Harley, granted, on mostly paved streets. She made Steve laugh out loud when she told him a hair-raising story about one of the dogs getting away, during her days as a dog walker when she first got to Southern California. Andi also shared a couple of her undercover sleuthing experiences while working as Mrs. Huber's assistant.

When they ran out of things to talk about, Steve asked, "So? What have you decided?"

"Let's do it," Andi said.

"It's a date! I'll get to your motel between 10:00 and 10:30."

Andi's last thought before falling asleep was, no big deal. Just some fun ridin' dirt bikes.

CHAPTER 39

R. A. began to extensively research the three organizations immediately after ending her phone conversation with Andi. Using several different search engines and a bit of imagination, she finally stumbled on their true proprietorship. Alzheimer's Research Field, Battlement for Cancer Institute, and God's Critters Foundation were all owned by TS Safe Investments. Googling "TS Safe Investments" put an immediate damper on her first enthusiasm. All she got was their financial adviser spiel on how to best invest one's money. Not making any more progress in further internet research, she decided to sleep on it.

Early Monday morning, she went for a brisk walk along the beach to mull things over. So all three philanthropic groups had the same owners. Interesting! But who was behind TS Safe Investments? That was the crux of the matter she needed to explore.

The executive director jogged by in his swim trunks on the way back from his morning dip in the ocean.

"Good morning, Mr. Beaulieu!" R. A. said.

He raised his hand in greeting, without losing his rhythm.

R. A. suddenly gave herself a mental slap and thought, off with the kid gloves, it's time I get aggressive. She turned on her heels and headed back to the community.

As soon as the dining room opened for breakfast, she joined Cheryl and Elaine at their table. The place filled up fast; everyone seemed to be up and hungry early on that day. Jim and Jane were busy chatting with Bill at a table immediately behind them. Straight ahead, Tom and Rose signed to each other, and Betty sat with Claudia next to them at a corner table for two. R. A. had never seen the staff members eating in the dining room before, but on that morning, they seemed to be having a meeting over breakfast at a large round table. The rest of the folks in the room were strangers to R. A.

Cheryl asked, "Where have you been hiding? We've missed you lately."

"I've been taking long walks, trying to sort out my life."

Cheryl and Elaine both looked puzzled and expected R. A. to elaborate.

When the latter stayed silent, Cheryl said, "What do you mean by 'sorting out your life'?"

R. A. made sure she talked loud enough for everyone in the room to hear when she stated, "My husband and I never made a will. Now that he passed on, it's time for me to draw one up. After all, I'm not getting any younger. But before I make an appointment with my lawyer, I need to figure out to whom to leave my money."

Elaine asked, "Don't you want your kids to inherit?"

"Of course, that goes without saying, but I'd like to leave a legacy to some charity organization. There are so many good causes; it's hard to make up my mind."

Having made her statement, R. A. suddenly concentrated on eating her bacon and eggs, and when she spoke again, she led the conversation in a different direction.

Later that morning, a phone call took place:
"Any luck with the room search?" the first person asked.
"None. I couldn't find a wallet with her I. D. She apparently keeps her identity hidden," the second replied.
"That fact makes her even more suspicious."
"I have bad vibes about her."
"I'm busy right now, but leave it to me. I'll find out who she is."
"No matter who the woman is, she's definitely on to us; I'm scared."
"What makes you think so?" the first person asked.
"She was fishing for someone to take the bait this morning at breakfast."
"What the devil are you talking about?"
"She shouted so everyone in the room could hear that she's planning to make a will and being undecided what charity she should name in it."
"Under no circumstances approach her on the subject! Act normal and harmless around her, do you hear?"
"Loud and clear."

Hours later, an individual entered one of Shore Haven's staff offices and asked, "Would it be any trouble to look up R. A.'s last name? I want to befriend her on Facebook."
"No trouble at all. Hang on a moment." The employee closed the file she had been working on and opened another. "Here we go. Her full name is Regula, Agatha Huber." And she read the line below aloud, "Generally goes by R. A. Huber."
"Thank you so much; you're a doll!"
"Anytime!"

CHAPTER 40

Steve showed up in Panguitch promptly at 10:15 and said, "You've had breakfast, right?"

"Hours ago," Andi replied.

"Good. Then let's get started."

Steve's manager friend said it was no problem when asked if Andy could leave her Harley in the motel parking lot for a few more hours and to safe keep her touring bag at the reception desk. That settled, Andi hopped into the pickup truck and they headed south along Highway 89, turned into a dirt road on the left, which took them past the dump, and soon reached the Casto Canyon trailhead.

Steve parked and unloaded the two dirt bikes, and as they strapped on their helmets, he asked, "Have you ever ridden on dirt roads before?"

"Some, but that was years ago."

"The trail we're taking is fairly easy; you should have no trouble," and he quickly explained the basics of a dirt bike, which Andi found not much different to handle from a regular motorcycle.

The first four miles wound up Casto Canyon Wash among spectacular red rock, sandstone cliffs of white, pink and green, some pinyon and cedar pines, and a burst of spring wildflowers.

When a panorama of red rock hoodoos came into view, Andi stopped her bike, planted her feet firmly on the ground, and exclaimed, "Holy Krewe! This is amazing."

"Told you there's plenty of hoodoos," he teased.

Soon the trail narrowed and ran over a clay-and-shale hill, which Andi found tricky to ride on, but in the end she managed without any mishap. She could imagine that this terrain would be slippery as hell after a rainstorm. Steve, always taking the lead, found the easiest passages for her. After she conquered that hill, he lifted one arm and gave her a thumbs-up. They reached the top of the plateau and took the dead-end trail to their left, which led out onto Casto Bluff overlook. They rested for a few minutes, taking in the view down to Panguitch and the Sevier Valley.

The adventure ride then took them through forested areas of ponderosa pines, where the colors of the landscape changed with every turn of the trail, and several passages across a dry riverbed. They continued on to Limekiln Canyon, on top of which stood an extensive row of bristlecone pines.

Steve stopped suddenly, waited for Andi to ride up by his side, and said "How about lunch?"

"You brought food?" Andi asked surprised.

"Not much, but it'll keep us going for a while."

They left the bikes on the trail and climbed a nearby boulder, where they found a comfortable spot to sit on. Steve took their lunch out of his fanny pack, consisting of an energy bar for each, some dried apricots, and a bottle of water to share.

While munching on their bars, he pointed at a bristlecone pine and stated, "These trees can live up to 5000 years, making them the oldest known individuals of any species. They do well in rocky soils, as you can see."

Andi swallowed a bite and remarked, "They sure look sturdy."

They lingered for a while after finishing their snacks and the tête-à-tête got more personal.

Andi said, "Tell me, what makes a news anchor give up suit and tie, picking dirt bike ridin' for a hobby?"

He grinned and replied, "It gives me balance. My work schedule can get hectic, especially when covering breaking news. Riding on dirt trails lifts up my soul, and at the same time, the sport is physically challenging. Today, I chose a mellow, relatively easy trail, but when I ride on my own or with my buddies, I wrestle with more hardcore stuff."

He gave her an approving look and continued, "You're doing great, though, and later on our 'homerun', there's enough downhill to make it a blast. You'll see!"

They talked about life in New Orleans, Southern California, Utah, and just life in general. Their exchange was easy, as if they had known each other for years.

Andi asked, "How come you still live with your folks?"

"For several reasons," he said, "but the main one is that I'm saving money so I can buy a house when I'm ready to settle down with the right person."

"Makes sense."

He touched her lightly on the shoulder and said, "You still miss the Big Easy, don't you?"

A faraway look came over her and she admitted, "I do get homesick, now and then. Have you been to New Orleans?"

"I covered a documentary there once, during Mardi Gras. It was one of the craziest, most fun experiences of my life!"

"No jivin'!"

"I could listen to your southern drawl forever and never get tired of it," he said, drawing her closer.

Andi pulled away and said, "Let's have none of that," jumping to her feet.

"Wait!" He got up too and asked, "Did I say something wrong?"

"Not at all, but romance is out of the question."

"You've had a bad experience and been hurt?"

"More than one, but that's not the point. After we get back to Panguitch, I'll be on my way to L.A. and you head back to Provo. I don't believe in long-distance relationships, and even less in one-night, or in this case, one-day stands."

"You sure tell it like it is!"

Back in the dirt-bike saddles, they stayed on the Limekiln Canyon trail until it looped to the west, and then all the way downward, making its way back to the Casto Canyon Trailhead. Steve was right; Andi got a rush on the downhill ride.

They were both subdued on the short truck drive to Panguitch. Steve thought, I found the perfect woman for me; my bad luck she lives in California. Andi thought, I probably hurt his feelings, but couldn't help it. At the motel, they both made a quick bathroom stop.

Then Steve asked, "How about a real lunch?"

Andi checked her watch and said, "It's past two o'clock already, so I had best head on south. I want to get to Hurricane before dark."

As he walked her to where the Harley-Davidson was parked, he said, "So this is it?" His blue eyes were full of regret.

"Guess so. Thank you! I had a blast."

He still stood next to her when she got on the Harley, then stared in amazement as she pulled him closer, making him bend down to her, and kissed him full on the lips. Then she quickly put her bike into gear and rode off, never looking back.

CHAPTER 41

Andi traveled the 124 miles from Panguitch to Hurricane via the Scenic Byway 12, which took her along unique and gorgeous landscapes, so that she was able to shake Steve from her mind and enjoy the moment. There was even a stretch along State Route 9 leading through part of Zion National Park. She had to buy a pass to ride through the park, which was still valid on the next day when she planned to take the shuttle bus into the park. Traffic was congested within the park, making for slow going, especially in the tunnels. It was past five o'clock when she rolled into Hurricane, under cloudy skies and the promise of rain in the air. She found lodging and asked if she could leave it open until the next morning whether to stay one or two nights, depending on the weather. "Sure you may," the nice lady at the reception desk assured her.

For dinner, she opted for Mexican food, avoiding the sudden downpour of heavy rain. By the time she had finished her meal of carnitas, the storm had eased a bit and she sprinted to her motel, beating the next deluge. Then she touched base with Mrs. Huber.

"Where are you?" the lady wanted to know.

"In Hurricane, where it's raining buckets."

"What are your plans?"

"I'd like to visit Zion without gettin' wet! If the storm is gone by tomorrow, I'll do some hikes in the park. If not, I reckon I'll head south in search of sunshine. What's up with you?"

R. A. said, "I was throwing some major hints on the table this morning and am now waiting for results." She relayed the tip-off to her breakfast audience at large.

"Let's hope our murderer takes the bait."

"How was Bryce Canyon?"

"I didn't make it to Bryce but had a blast dirt bike ridin' with Steve, Fred's grandson." And she told of her Casto Canyon trail adventures.

"I get the feeling that you like that young man!" said R. A.

"Yes, ma'am. I sure do. I'd best put him out of my mind, though, him living in Provo, Utah, and all."

"Is he Mormon?"

"I don't know; religion didn't come up."

On that note, they ended the call.

Andi woke up to a blue sky and sunshine on Tuesday morning. Zion National Park, here I come, she told herself. Zion was a 25-mile ride from Hurricane. She parked the Harley in the small town of Springdale, then took the shuttle into the park. She had a glorious day with perfect weather, sunny but not hot. The orange and cream peaks of rock formation and vast canyons were highly impressive. Amazing what nature had formed in thousands of years.

The shuttle dropped her off at the end station, Temple Sinewave, where she went for a hike along the river, leading to the Narrows. She was one hiker among many. That particular stretch by the stream seemed to be popular with tourists. Still, she found a spot by the riverbed away from the crowd, sat down on a log, took the sandwich she had bought in Hurricane out of her touring bag, and had a picnic lunch. She then took the shuttle back down and exited at several stations to take pictures and enjoy the magnificent rock panorama. At the Grotto stop, she opted for another hike. This trail was steep and at times narrow, with fewer trekkers. She endured all the way to the top, panting but feeling accomplished when she arrived at the crest.

Toward early evening, as she rode back to Hurricane Andi thought, Zion was magnificent; I am a lucky woman to have experienced it. She woke up at the crack of dawn on Wednesday and decided to tackle the 405 miles in one day, all the way home.

CHAPTER 42

Meanwhile, R. A. mulled over her question: Who owns TS Safe Investments? Something nagged at the back of her mind, but she could not put her finger on it. "What am I missing?" she burst out.

The lady detective happened to be on one of her walks on the ocean front path, and Charley, who strode a few paces behind her said, "Be more specific."

She turned around and came face to face with the former physicist. "Oh, hi Charley. I was just thinking aloud."

"Watch out, soon they may tag you as crazy too!"

They both laughed at his joke.

Then he said, "You're the initial lady, R. A. Correct?"

"You got it."

"Using initials for everyone instead of names would sure make it easier on people's memory."

"Yes and no," she argued. "One would soon mix up the letters."

They chatted some more, but she barely paid attention. Her thoughts were stuck on initials. Of course, she mused, TS! They have the same last name. Why didn't that occur to me sooner? She abruptly made an excuse to Charley, spun around, and hurried back toward Shore Haven.

Charley, who had been cut off in mid-sentence, thought, what an airhead! And I'm the one diagnosed with dementia.

In her room, R. A. went straight to her laptop and performed a final round of research. "Bingo!" she exclaimed, and shut the computer down.

At that moment, another secret phone conversation took place.

Person number one said, "I found their website. R. A. and the redhead who poses as her niece are private investigators."

"We're in trouble!"

"Don't worry, I have a plan to eliminate them both. I created something months ago in case of a major problem."

"Tell me already! I'm on pins and needles," person number two implored.

"Not over the phone. I'll talk to you in person. In the meantime, I'll have to act fast, before the sleuth figures out what we're about."

"I'm scared!"

"Stop being such a wuss. I've got it under control, so pull yourself together."

CHAPTER 43

At her office in Pasadena on Thursday morning, Andi tended to mail and phone messages that had accumulated during the week she had been out of town. She responded to a possible new client inquiry first, and then was about to call Mrs. Huber, letting her know that she was home, when the business phone rang.

"Ms. LeJeune, this is Dave Beaulieu. I'm afraid I have bad news. Your aunt has suddenly taken ill."

"What do you mean by 'taken ill'?" Andi shouted into the phone.

"The doctor doesn't know what ails her, but it's serious."

"I'm on my way!" Andi yelled and hung up.

She threw her smartphone and Derringer pistol into the touring bag and flew out the door. Riding in the diamond lane wherever possible and mostly speeding, she was lucky not to get stopped and ticketed by a highway patrol officer. During the entire trip to Ventura, all sorts of scenarios raced through her mind. The killer had obviously caught on to Mrs. Huber and attempted to silence her. What did 'suddenly taken ill' and the doctor not knowing what was wrong mean? Was Mrs. Huber poisoned? Did the bastard tamper with her blood pressure medication? Had she been struck unconscious and suffered a concussion? Useless to speculate.

She thought, should I have let Mr. Huber know? Mercy! Mr. Huber is gonna skin me alive if something happens to his missus. I should've stayed put and protected her, instead of gallivanting all over Utah. Then she realized how irrational that self-accusation was. Besides, her former boss had been in tight spots before and knew how to take care of herself. And then another realization popped into her head. Granted, Mrs. Huber had listed her as the contact person, but would she have given out the business phone number rather than her cellphone?

As she rode into Shore Haven's underground garage with a pounding heart and sick to her stomach, she said a silent prayer: "Please, God, let her be okay!"

She spotted Mrs. Huber's Volkswagen Passat and parked the Harley next to it, took off her helmet, and was in the process of hoisting her touring bag when something hit her from behind and she was instantly locked tight into the sling of a rope with her arms firmly pressed against her body. She let go of the touring bag, which fell to the ground. When she tried to move, the rope was pulled tighter. Even before her antagonist stepped forward from behind Mrs. Huber's car, she heard his nasty laugh.

"Another one of my magic tricks," he announced as he got closer. "My own version of throwing a lasso."

After the initial shock of being tied up and the realization of who the enemy was, Andi needed to think fast. She said, "What the heck, Todd, are you tryin' to be funny?" doing her best to sound unconcerned, but knowing that she was in mortal danger. Keeping up a conversation may be her best chance.

"So it was *you* who called and not Mr. Beaulieu! Betcha R. A. is not sick at all."

"Smart of you to catch on," he said, full of sarcasm. "But enough talk."

Andi tried to ease her foot closer to where her touring bag lay, but Todd noticed and picked it up himself. He opened it, glanced inside, and noticed the Derringer, as well as her phone.

He did his revolting laugh again and commented, "Just like I expected, you came prepared."

In the next second, he had her loaded pistol in his right hand, pointing it at her temple, while fiddling with her phone with his left. "What do you have R. A.'s number listed under? Tell me, quick," he said, while pressing the gun tighter to her head.

"Under 'boss'," Andi replied.

"Okay. After I dial, you tell her that you need to show her something in the car, and make sure she brings the keys. No monkey business, or I pull the trigger."

"Let me get my arm out of the rope so I can hold the phone."

"You think I'm stupid and let you talk in private?" He pulled the rope even tighter, making her totally immobile. She was glad she was wearing her leather jacket, or it would have cut her blood circulation.

He put the phone on speaker mode and pressed "boss."

"Hello Andi! Are you back from your trip?"

"Hi there, Regula! I had a great old time."

Todd made a cut-throat gesture with his hand, letting her know to stop the chitchat.

"Where are you now?" R. A. asked.

"Actually, I'm in the Shore Haven garage, right by your car. Can you come here for a sec? I need to show you somethin'."

"I can't leave right now. Come to my apartment first."

Todd shook his head.

"Sorry, Regula, what I have to show you is in your car. Don't forget the keys."

"It will take a while, then. I just stepped out of the shower and need to dress and blow dry my hair."

Todd shook his head again vigorously, and Andi could tell he was going to lose his cool at any moment. The pistol at her temple was a steady reminder that he meant business.

Andi said, "Never mind the hair; this is urgent. Come as fast as you can."

Todd cut the line and said, "So far you've been cooperative. Keep it up, or you'll regret it."

They heard a car driving into the garage, and Todd shoved Andi behind R. A.'s car, against the wall, and then lowered the pistol and dug it into her side while keeping her hidden behind his own body. When Jim and Jane stepped out of their SUV some distance away and walked toward the elevator, he waved to them, and they waved a greeting back.

When they were out of sight, Andi said, "I see you're keepin' up the reputation."

"What the hell are you talking about?"

She gestured upward with her head in the direction of the community building and stated, "You're known among the old folks a nice young man."

He did not comment.

Andi continued, "Did you have to twist Elaine's arm to get her to play along, or is she a willing criminal? And while we're on the subject, is she really your aunt?"

Angry now, he replied, "She's smart enough to grab an opportunity when it comes along, and for your information, we are blood related. She *is* my aunt, which is more than I can say about your relationship with R. A. Huber."

"So you've figured out her last name and know who we are?"

"Brilliant of you to finally get the drift!" He nudged the gun harder into her side and said, "Now shut up. We're going to wait for the old sleuth in silence," and he made another phone call, this one from his own phone.

CHAPTER 44

R. A. Huber assumed that Andi had arrived home late on the night before and might want to sleep in on Thursday morning. She anticipated a phone call from her, eager to let her know that the case was solved in her mind, and that now they needed to look for proof. The chat with Charley had triggered her sudden brainstorm of tying the initials TS to Todd. Elaine had mentioned that Todd was her brother's son during one of their conversations, and Andi's background check on Elaine revealed that she went back to her maiden name after the divorce, which was "Singer." So it followed that her nephew's name was Todd Singer.

Googling "Todd Singer" exposed him as the owner of TS Safe Investments. Andi had only done background checks on residents and staff members of Shore Haven. Who would have thought to check on visitors? Now, of course, they needed to find out who did which murders. It seemed that Todd was most likely the person who drowned Kitty, pretending to give her swimming lessons, and Elaine may have been the "in house" person, eliminating Norma and Fred. The motive was greed, pure and simple.

That the three charitable organizations were linked to TS Safe Investments, owned by Todd, was evidence that he benefited from the deaths of three people - - maybe even more - - and the probability of a scam and "undue influence" was evident. The question was how evidence could be obtained to prove that murder had been committed. She and Andi needed to figure that out, before getting the authorities involved.

When the phone rang, seeing that the call came from Andi, she answered it full of enthusiasm. Not in a million years would Andi ever call R. A. Huber by her first name, so when she heard her say "Regula", knew right away that something was wrong. Under different circumstances, the way Andi pronounced the name would have been comical, but the situation was dead serious. She had to assume that Andi was held hostage by either Todd or Elaine, or possibly both. She also supposed that the phone was set on speaker, therefore, she had needed to talk with utmost caution.

Stalling with her pretense of coming out of the shower and needing more time had not worked, so they expected her in the garage within minutes. She first called 911 - - ironically admitting to herself that she needed to involve the police sooner than planned - - explaining that she and Andi were in danger of their lives. She related her location, making sure they understood that the confrontation was taking place in the underground garage. She added, "There is a good possibility that the villain will force us into a ride in my own car," and gave them her license plate number. She stressed, "This is urgent; please hurry." Then she opened the safe, took out her wallet, keys, and the loaded .25 pistol, and stashed the items in her purse.

When R. A. stepped out of the elevator, arms extended, holding the pistol with both hands, cautiously advancing toward her VW, Todd ordered, "Drop the gun!" still aiming the Derringer directly at Andi. R. A. lowered her pistol, holding it in one hand only. "Drop it to the ground, dammit, or she gets it first!" he yelled, motioning toward Andi with his head. R. A. did as she was told.

"Now open the car door and get in," he ordered.

R. A. fumbled with the keys and dropped them.

Todd was furious, and, kicking her pistol out of reach, he said, "Don't try any more tricks, and stop the delaying tactics. Open the car doors and get in." It was clear the man's nerves were at a breaking point as he shouted, "This has taken way too long already."

R. A. clicked the doors open and got into the driver seat, while Todd shoved Andi into the back seat.

Both car doors stood wide open, and when he made no move to walk around the vehicle and get into the passenger side or join Andi in the back, R. A. asked, "Aren't you going to ride shotgun?"

He laughed his evil laugh but said nothing.

"We're not going for a ride?"

He was finally coaxed into showing off how clever he felt and stated, "You are going nowhere. This is end-of-trail for you!"

Both ladies knew that their only hope was to keep him talking. R. A. expected the police to show up, and Andi was hoping that other folks would appear in the garage, either parking or leaving, rather sooner than later.

So Andi said, "How are y'all goin' to manage that?"

"I guess it doesn't hurt to let you know, since you're not going to live to tell about it. Months ago, I prepared a device in case it would come in handy someday. Well, it's attached to the bottom of the VW now."

"Holy Krewe! We're sittin' on a bomb."

The elevator bell sounded, putting all three on alert. Elaine stepped off and hurried to the scene.

"About time you showed," her nephew said.

"I couldn't get away from Cheryl right away."

"You're here now, so let's not waste any more time. Pick up that gun from the ground and cover the old woman while I set to work." He produced more rope and tied Andi's feet together, then made R. A. Huber's arms and legs immobile too.

Confident that neither woman could move, he tossed Andi's gun and phone back into her touring bag and told Elaine to add R. A.'s pistol to the collection, then placed the bag on the passenger seat.

R. A. said, "Your fingerprints are on those weapons and Andi's phone. Shouldn't you wipe them off?"

He thought about it for a second, then said, "They'll go up in flames. And now, no more delay!"

He pointed at Elaine, saying, "Hurry up and get out of here. Go to the lounge and make sure you're seen by plenty of people in the next few minutes."

"What about you?" Andi argued. "You'll be right here when the thing goes off!"

He let lose his repulsive laugh for the last time and said, "That's where today's wonderful technology comes into play. I'll be heading south on the freeway when I activate the device from my smartphone."

About to close both car doors and walk away, he said, "Oh, I almost forgot! I can't have you screaming," and taped a rag over Andi's mouth.

He was in the process of gagging R. A. too, when all hell broke loose. The Ventura police drove into the garage in full force, coming to the private investigators' rescue in the nick of time. Todd tried to make a run for it, but the officers wrestled him to the ground, reciting him his rights while snapping closed the handcuffs.

On later examination, the authorities did indeed find a lethal device attached to Huber's car, which was programmed to be activated with Todd's phone. The two private eyes spent a good part of the day giving their statements at the Ventura Police station, prompting the arrest of Elaine.

EPILOGUE

At the end of October, Dave Beaulieu called all residents and staff members of Shore Haven together for a meeting in the lounge.

He addressed the assembly with, "I'm sure you've heard or read about the Singer murder trial. The court case ended yesterday with a conviction for both Todd and Elaine Singer of embezzlement and first degree murder. Since the horrendous acts of those two individuals concern us all here in our community, I have invited two ladies who testified as witnesses at the trial to speak to you about what happened here at the beginning of the year. One of them lived among us under cover, the other posed as her niece. They did not even take me into their confidence at the time, but they are private investigators."

He waved them into the room and said, "Here they are, R. A. Huber and Antoinette LeJeune."

Huber started her talk with, "The obvious reason we had to keep everyone in the dark was because we considered all of you as suspects." She spotted Rose in a front-row seat of her audience and addressed her in sign language, "I'll speak slowly so that you can read my lips."

She continued, "Andi and I figured out who the culprits were, the motive, and how the murders were committed, but the details came out in the trial. Elaine seemed remorseful and signed a confession. Here is the gist of the matter. The planning of the scheme took place even before Elaine came to live at Shore Haven. By the way, she was only 64 when she first joined your community, which should have raised a red flag, but we missed it. One day, she mentioned to her nephew that she was envious of the rich people who could afford to live out their golden years at Shore Haven. Todd told her that he could make it happen, but she needed to trust him and follow his orders. I'm sure those of you who know her are aware that she adored her nephew and was putty in his hands. So he thought out a ruse to capitalize on residents, made Elaine quit her beautician job, and enrolled her at Shore Haven. He named himself as responsible for her month-to-month rent, listing his legitimate investment company as collateral.

"Having Elaine planted among residents, he instructed her to target her peers. He was clever enough to make her wait until she was well established before finding out where their interests lay and then suggest leaving a legacy in their wills to the appropriate organizations. He first made her approach the oldest resident," Huber smiled toward Betty, "but instead of reaching her goal, she earned the scorn of that lady. When targeting some others, Elaine made progress, and Todd profited as they died. Oh, yes, the first few victims to his scam died natural deaths." She nodded at Bill, "Your mixed-doubles tennis partner was among them."

Then she motioned to the redhead standing next to her and said, "Let Andi tell you about the discoveries she made on a trip to Reno, Nevada, and Provo, Utah."

Andi told what she had learned from Norma and Fred's sons and how disappointed she first felt when realizing that Norma and Fred's wills benefited totally different charities than that of Kitty Ralph's. The Singer trial revealed that Mrs. Huber's exploration had been correct: Alzheimer's Research Field, Battlement for Cancer Institute, and God's Critters Foundation, were all linked to TS Safe Investments, owned by Todd. The man was not only a magician but knew how to juggle financial assets around. After the funds were transferred, he dissolved the respective philanthropic organizations and created new ones.

She pointed at Cheryl and stated, "We have reason to believe that you'd have been the next target; he created a new account in March by the name of Comrades of Theater."

Cheryl burst out, "I knew that we had a killer among us, but Elaine! I thought she was my friend."

Andi continued her narrative, saying that Todd's scam had worked, but when he got even greedier and decided that folks didn't die fast enough on their own, things got out of hand. Knowing that he had a short amount of time before the IRS or anyone else caught on, he told Elaine that they needed to help these residents along. At first, his aunt was appalled at the idea of killing people, but Todd brainwashed her into thinking that the old folks' days were numbered anyway. They might have gotten away with murdering Norma and Fred, but Kitty's drowning made her son and daughter-in-law suspicious of foul play, resulting in Mr. Ralph hiring her services.

When Andi came to a halt, Mr. Beaulieu said, "I have a question. Who did the actual killings?"

R. A. Huber took over. "Kitty was drowned by Todd, who was good at manipulating people. He made her believe that she would get a swimming lesson but pushed her into the elements instead. Elaine murdered the other two victims, instructed by Todd as to the exact manner," and she related the story of nail and twine on top of the flight of stairs, in Norma's murder. As to Fred, she explained, "Todd taught Elaine how to pick a lock. She waited until late one night when her prey was asleep, sneaked into his room, and smothered him with his own pillow. Then she placed it back underneath his head, making it appear that the man died in his sleep."

Claudia spoke up. "Elaine approached me too, more than a year ago, asking if I had made my last will and testament. I cut her short before she had a chance to elaborate and threatened her with legal action if she didn't leave me alone."

Charley raised his hand and said, "I have a question too. You said that Elaine confessed. What about Todd? Did he also sign a confession?"

"No, he pleaded not guilty, alleging that Elaine's confession had been obtained under duress and that she was mentally incompetent. The jury convicted him of the crimes, though. That's what counts." And she added, "It is possible that Elaine did not confess out of remorse but to get a lesser sentence."

"What were the sentences?" Charley wanted to know.

Andi said, "We don't know yet. The sentencing hearing has yet to take place. I reckon that Todd gets the maximum of either life in prison without the possibility of parole, or worse." She turned to R. A. and asked, "What's your guess about Elaine's sentence, Mrs. Huber?"

"I would assume at least life in prison, which at her age means that she will never see the outside world again."

When R. A. Huber arrived home and told Peter about the speech she and Andi had given at the retirement community, he said, "I hope that this was your final active case and that you'll never again see the inside of Shore Haven."

"Your wish is granted. I'm not planning to physically work on any more cases." She chuckled and added, "As for Shore Haven, maybe you'll hit it big with a bestseller so that we can both enjoy the rest of our golden years at the facility!"

A few days later, Andi answered a call:

"Hey Andi! It's Steve."

Her heart skipped a couple of beats and she didn't respond straight away.

"Steve, from the dirt bike ride in Casto Canyon, remember?"

"Oh, that Steve, I plumb forgot!" she teased.

"Listen, I took what you said about long-distance relationships seriously."

"Yeah?"

"Today, I had a job interview for an anchor position with a TV station in Southern California and made the cut. I'll move down next week!"

"No jivin'?"

"No jivin'!" he repeated.

"I'm tickled pink!" Andi said, and did a little dance of pure joy.

Stand-Alone Mystery by Alice Zogg

A Bet Turned Deadly

R. A. Huber Mysteries by Alice Zogg

Evil at Shore Haven
Guilty or Not
Murder at the Cubbyhole
Revamp Camp
Final Stop Albuquerque
The Fall of Optimum House
The Lonesome Autocrat
Tracking Backward
Turn the Joker Around
Reaching Checkmate

Available at www.amazon.com,
www.barnesandnoble.com
and other vendors.